The Girl's Insidious Shadow

The Eternal Night Saga, Volume 2

Patrick Luther

Published by Patrick Luther, 2023.

THE GIRL'S INSIDIOUS SHADOW

First edition. September 26, 2023.

Copyright © 2023 Patrick Luther.

ISBN: 979-8988771005

Written by Patrick Luther.

Prologue: Death of Innocence

Little Cassie had been at the orphanage for three long years before she was finally adopted by Kaleb and Darcy Ebonwood. Most of that time had been spent missing her family, struggling with night terrors about how she lost them, but it rapidly receded once she found a new family. Life at the orphanage hadn't been bad, but it was lonely. Cassie had not felt loved there, but Kaleb and Darcy never missed a chance to remind her how happy they were to have her.

Eventually, Cassie learned her new mom couldn't carry a child of her own, and Kaleb and Darcy had decided on adoption. Over the seven years Cassie had been with them, she had even begun to feel as though they were her real parents—they kept her fed and warm, and she had no shortage of toys to keep her occupied. However, Cassie struggled to make friends at school. The other kids seemed to find her impeccable manners and sharp observation skills off-putting, but that was okay.

She truly only needed *one* friend.

Cassie's shadow was her only company in her bedroom as she tried on dresses she had received for her thirteenth birthday. Along with the dresses, her mom had gotten her a standing full body mirror, and Cassie admired herself in it as she swapped one dress for another. First was a long black gown with rhinestone straps, then a royal blue empire dress followed by a brilliant red babydoll style with glitter in the lacy skirt.

She fluttered the eyelashes over her deep blue eyes, smiling brilliantly and admiring each dress. Her mom had said Cassie was growing into a fine young lady, and Cassie was enjoying every second of it and how pretty the new clothes made her feel. Each dress went perfectly with her smooth, porcelain skin, long black hair, and blooming hourglass figure. She grinned delightedly, spinning in what might have been her favorite dress from the bunch—a lavender sundress with embroidered violets along the hem.

Cassie paused to look herself up and down, her face flushing slightly. Her mom had also told her, "I wish I had been as beautiful at your age as you are." Though Cassie didn't normally look at herself that way, while she examined herself in the dress, her mom's words echoed in her mind. *I am pretty.* She smiled at her reflection, joy and pride lighting her face up as she turned back toward the pile to see what was next.

"Lock the door."

Cassie's smile faltered when the soft, dry voice whispered in her ear, accompanied by a sudden chill in the air. "Why?" she said softly, completely accustomed to the cold marking her friend's presence.

"Just do it," he insisted.

Though perplexed, Cassie trusted her friend. She walked over to the door and turned the lock on the knob. Cassie frowned at it for a second, but then the knob suddenly turned, and someone pushed hard against the door, as though they had expected it to open. Cassie jumped back, nearly exclaiming in fright.

Her dad's voice called from the other side. "Cassie? Is everything all right?"

She furrowed her brow, and a chill that had nothing to do with her friend ran down her spine. However, her voice was steady when she replied, "Everything's fine, Dad. Just trying on some dresses."

"Oh," he replied simply, then asked, "Sure you don't want a second opinion?"

Maybe I do. However, before Cassie could even start toward the door, she felt it—her friend's presence once more—and it was neither calm nor curious. It felt...threatening? *What is it?*

"Be wary of him," he whispered in her ear.

"Why?" Cassie kept her focus on the door, still puzzled.

"He's starting to see you differently."

"Cassie?" her dad asked.

Not realizing how long she and her friend had held their mumbled conversation, Cassie tried to think of something to say. Her friend's presence bristled, but she decided to ignore it.

"Just a second, Dad." Cassie stepped back over to the door, unlocked the knob, and opened it. "Come on in!"

Her dad stood in the doorway for a moment, appraising her. Kaleb was a tall man with a round nose and cheeks showing only the slightest hint of both age and fat. He was not a large man, but Kaleb often joked about years of fast food slowly catching up to him in his old age. His hair was light and thinning down the center, and his beady, pale-blue eyes glowed with warmth.

"Looking pretty good, Cass!"

"Thanks, Daddy!" Cassie tittered excitedly and spun on the spot. She stepped over in front of the mirror once more, her hands swishing the skirt around. "I think this one is my favorite."

"I can see why," her dad observed, stepping up behind her. "Might I offer a suggestion, though?"

Cassie paused her swaying. "What's that?"

"Try letting the straps hang off of your shoulders."

Cassie frowned. "Why?"

Her dad shrugged. "Just try it and see."

"Okay," Cassie said, suddenly strangely uncomfortable.

Still, there was nothing to fear. He was her father, after all. Slowly, Cassie slipped the straps of the dress off from each shoulder and looked at herself in the mirror.

"You see?" her dad asked.

Cassie shrugged, frowning. "Not really."

"It makes you look a little more mature."

Cassie looked at her face, tracing her neckline to her now bare shoulders. The only thing keeping the dress in place was her already ample bust, but one wrong move might cause it to slip.

"You're growing into a gorgeous young woman, honey," her dad said with pride, resting his hand on her shoulder.

Cassie smiled, but then she looked at her dad's reflection in the mirror. He was grinning, but his beady eyes were not on hers. His thumb stroked her bare back gently, then his eyes fell on her chest.

Another shiver ran up Cassie's spine. Suddenly fighting the urge to panic, she said, "Well, thanks, Dad! I gotta get changed, though."

Her dad blinked and shook his head as if to clear it. He turned toward the door. "Right, right! I'll leave you to it, then."

Once her dad was gone, Cassie locked the door again and backed up to the bed. There was something deeply disturbing about the way her dad had looked at her. The way he had stroked her back, his eyes trailing across her bare skin, left her with a sudden urge to take a scalding shower.

"He is starting to see you differently," her friend repeated.

"Differently how?" Cassie asked nervously, turning to gaze at herself in the mirror. The straps of the sundress still hung around her shoulders. With a puzzled expression, she gave the skirt of the dress a tug, and as predicted, it fell into a pile at her feet.

Cassie looked herself up and down, truly seeing herself for the first time. Same pale complexion, same jet-black hair and shining blue eyes—so why would her dad be starting to see her differently? What could have changed?

As Cassie thought about it, her eyes fell from her confused face to her well-developed bare chest, to the curves of her waist and hips. A shudder of revulsion ran along her spine. Suddenly, she felt far too exposed and moved her arms to cover herself.

Cassie shook her head. "You're wrong. I'm his daughter."

"Be careful around him," the voice whispered earnestly.

Cassie bristled, another shiver racing down her back, but she waved a hand dismissively. "You're just being overcautious. He would never do anything to hurt me." Still, Cassie couldn't get the image of his wandering eyes out of her head. She was done trying on dresses for the night, so she threw on a T-shirt and sat down on her bed to read. For the rest of the night, her door remained locked.

"There have been other times," her friend pressed.

"No there haven't...," Cassie replied huffily, but her voice trailed off as she recalled an incident just a few days earlier when her dad had blundered into the bathroom while she was getting out of the shower. At the time, she had assumed it was an honest accident, but his eyes had lingered on her naked body just a little too long, even after she had covered herself with a towel. Before that, she had dropped a fork on the floor when they were loading the dishwasher together. As she bent over to pick it up, she caught him staring at her rear...or did she? She might have only imagined it, but with the idea in her head, she couldn't be sure. "You're making me paranoid," Cassie grumbled.

"We shall see," her friend whispered in reply.

TWO NIGHTS LATER, CASSIE stirred from her sleep. The air around her was unusually cold, despite the heavy blanket she slept under. That could only mean one thing…

Sure enough, her friend's presence filled the room, and it was angry. Very, very angry.

"What's going on?" Her voice was shaky as she sat up in the dark.

A muffled grunt from the direction of her door was the only reply. Puzzled, Cassie started to slide toward the edge of the bed to go to the light switch, but her friend got there first and clicked it on. Cassie's blood froze.

"D-d-d-Dad?"

Kaleb looked back at her from against the wall, his feet dangling about a foot from the floor. He was in his plain navy-blue pajamas and a black bathrobe. Shadowy tendrils enwrapped his arms and torso, with another around his mouth.

No. It can't be.

"Dad, what's going on?" Cassie asked, her voice cracking and tears filling her eyes.

"Do you believe me now?" her friend hissed.

Cassie wasn't able to. It couldn't be true. But even as he was held suspended by her friend, her dad's eyes darted toward her chest. The black nighty she wore had a V-cut neckline just low enough to show a generous amount of her cleavage. Cassie's heart shattered, and she clutched her blankets to her chest, tears spilling from her eyes.

"Daddy…why?"

Cassie's dad tried to answer, but her friend's tendril reduced it to a muffled grunt. Her dad shifted his wide eyes back to Cassie's, pleading. However, the pain in those eyes couldn't touch the pain building in her chest. She buried her face in the blankets and sobbed openly, unable to contain her sense of loss and betrayal. *He had been right all along.* The man she had come to think of as a father was actually a monster who craved the flesh of his own daughter. Her mind raced over their every memory together, from hosting tea parties to coming up with names for her stuffed animals, and everything in between. It all turned sour, crushed by the reality of how he now saw her.

Anger surged through Cassie. She looked up at the man she had called "Dad" with blazing eyes, her gritted teeth bared in a grimace of barely contained fury. Cassie wanted to hurt him. She wanted his pain to match her own. Her knuckles were white from how tightly she clutched the blanket to her chest, but they longed to clutch his throat in its place.

"We need him alive...for now," her friend warned.

Cassie winced. "You were right. You were right all along."

"Now listen here...," her friend hissed, turning his attention back to his captive.

He was whispering instructions, but Cassie didn't care to listen. She stared at the floor below her dad's bare feet, shaking as hot tears flowed freely down her cheeks. A part of her longed for a mere minute ago, when she had been oblivious to her would-be father's sickening desires. Another part wanted nothing less than to bury a knife in his gut.

I'm supposed to be able to trust him. If I can't, who can *I trust?* The thought brought a fresh wave of anguish over her, and she buried her face in her blanket again.

I can trust Asmodeous. He had tried to warn her, but she hadn't wanted to believe him. Still, she couldn't deny that he had tried. If not for him, who knew what her dad...no, what *Kaleb* would have done to her as she slept? What would she have woken up to? The thought made Cassie want to puke. *I'm gonna listen to him from now on. If I can't trust anyone else, at least I can trust Asmodeous.*

Cassie's bedroom door snapped shut, and she looked up. Kaleb was gone, but the gently writhing shadows still lingered on her wall. A tendril reached out to the doorknob and turned the lock. Another flicked the light switch, plunging them into pitch darkness.

Asmodeous's presence dissipated. He was back in Cassie's shadow, where he had lived for ten years now. Her friend was with her at all times and did not normally extend his presence beyond it...until now. *I will never doubt him again.*

Then Cassie heard Asmodeous's voice in her head. *We will begin training tomorrow.*

Training? she questioned.

It would be best if you learned how to defend yourself, Asmodeous clarified.

I understand.

Seemingly satisfied, Asmodeous fell silent, leaving Cassie alone with her thoughts. If she had felt leaving the bed was safe, she would have grabbed herself a shirt and pants to cover up with. She had loved her nighty, but now, it just made her feel too exposed to sleep. In fact, she was certain she would get no more sleep that night and for the next few nights to come.

Cassie eventually lay back down in her bed, still clutching her blankets to her chest, her mind once again running away with her. Seven years of happy memories, all tainted. What had once brought her joy now only brought her agony and hate.

Then Cassie recalled a particularly recent memory. Kaleb had written in a card for her thirteenth birthday that she was growing into a beautiful young woman. Cassie's gut twisted, and her heart clenched. Fresh tears spilled from her eyes, soaking both her hair and pillow as she stared up at the ceiling.

I hope no one calls me beautiful ever again.

1. Nerd Herd

"You know, there was a time I thought I was good at this game," Adam Sullivan grunted in exasperation, setting his controller down beside him on the sofa. He still fixed his brown eyes on the television screen, even though he had just been eliminated. Adam leaned back on the cushions and ran a thin, pale hand through his short, dark brown hair in defeat. *Calm down. It's just a game.*

Walter Tomsen was on his feet, controller in hand. He laughed and teased, "Time for a new champ, my friend." Walter bobbed back and forth as he played, and his open, button-down, short-sleeve shirt and baggy cargo pants flopped about, exaggerating his movements comically. "Dammit!" he exclaimed when he lost a life.

"Don't let your guard down, Walt." Damien Darquis leaned forward, seated cross-legged in front of the TV. His pale blue eyes never left the screen, and his tanned, round face split into a smug grin, a toothpick jutting out of the corner of his mouth. Damien gained the upper hand.

"Guard *this*!" Walter taunted, his lanky arms mimicking the punches his character was throwing in the game.

"Shit!" Damien gritted his teeth, crunching the toothpick between them.

"Don't get too cocky, Walt," Lex Volk warned as he, too, leaned forward in his rocking-chair seat opposite the room from Adam. Walter cursed once more when Lex took another of his lives, and Lex shot Adam a grin. "Consider yourself avenged."

Adam returned the smile but heaved a sigh. "Still can't believe I was the first to die."

"We all have bad days." Lex turned his smoky blue eyes back to the screen.

Walter nudged Lex's shoulder-length brown hair with an elbow. "You're gonna have a bad day if you don't focus!"

Lex's muscular shoulders rose and fell as he took a deep breath. "Could say the same about you."

"Sometimes, I think you guys take this game way too seriously." Ken Wolff snickered softly, sitting immediately to Adam's left in a large recliner angled to face the TV. A smile played across his thin face framed by shoulder-length brown hair, while the guys fought back and forth in their virtual shenanigans.

Adam, his pride wounded, sighed. "I know I do." He folded his arms across his chest, covering the band logo on his black T-shirt, and crossed his legs in their black denim jeans.

Walter chuckled. "Maybe that's why I can beat you now."

Adam shot a playful glare at him. "In the last game, I destroyed you every time."

"Yeah, but I made you work for it."

"Still kicked your ass in the end, though."

"If it was a *real* fight, that would be a different story," Ken interjected. Despite Damien being larger and Lex being more muscular, Ken was easily the toughest-looking of the bunch in his biker boots, tattered jeans, and spiked-denim vest. No one replied to his taunt, however.

"*Yes!*" Walter exclaimed.

Damien and Lex groaned and fought frantically to escape Walter's video game rampage. Within seconds, the game was over, and Walter danced victoriously.

Lex rolled his eyes. "There's such a thing as being a sore winner too, you know."

"Who says I'm dancing 'cause I won? Maybe I just wanna dance!" Walter retorted.

"Then why are you doing your so-called 'Victory Dance?'" Adam fired back.

Walter froze and held up a finger, his mouth agape as if to say something back, then slumped over in defeat.

Damien smirked. "Busted."

All five of them laughed aloud, then Adam turned to Ken and offered him the controller. "Want in on the next round?"

Ken waved the controller away. "I'm good. Y'all go ahead and kill each other."

"With pleasure." Adam grinned, taking hold of the controller once more and turning back to the TV.

The sound of the kitchen door opening gave him pause, followed by his mother's voice. "I got pizza!"

"Ceasefire!" Walter set his controller down and made for the dining room.

The rest of the gang did the same, following Walter from the living room, with its motif of burgundy and dark oak, through an entryway and into the brightly lit dining area. As Adam entered, he caught sight of his mother across the island counter separating the dining room from the kitchen.

Adam's mother, Patty, was a short, plump woman with wavy, brown locks and matching eyes behind her bifocals. She wore a T-shirt and blue jeans—her usual summer get-up—and carried two large pizza boxes. Patty set the boxes down on the island and opened them, filling the room with the smell of tomato sauce and sausage.

"I'll grab plates!" Adam volunteered, opening a cabinet in the dining room to pull out a stack of paper plates.

"Thank you," she said gratefully.

Adam distributed the plates to his friends before they dove at the pizza, grabbing two slices each. Once everyone else, including his mother, had their food, Adam finally grabbed a couple of slices for himself. The five boys stood around the table, enjoying the surprise pizza. Adam's mother ate in the kitchen, letting the boys be.

After several minutes, Ken asked, "So what's the plan for the Halloween party this year?"

Walter, Lex, and Damien all looked at Adam. Since he and his family had just moved into the new house over the summer, the future of their annual Halloween party would be unclear.

Adam finished a bite of his pizza, then explained, "Of course, it's still happening. Halloween is on a Saturday this year, so that will be the day. Since it's our first year out here, we'll take guests on a walk around the field and woods, then ambush them on their way back to the house. We can prep in the barn."

Damien grinned fiendishly, folding his arms across his tank-top-covered chest. "Me likey."

Walter asked, "So who is gonna be what?"

"Well, I wanted to leave that up to you guys," Adam replied with a shrug.

"I'll lead the walk," Ken volunteered.

"Not much for scaring people?" Walter raised an eyebrow.

Ken smirked. "It's fun, but I laugh too easily."

"So, while the rest of us are acting like psychotic freaks, you'll be rolling on the ground, laughing?" Adam mused aloud.

"Depends on how dramatic people are,"

"Someone will cry. Someone always does," Walter said gleefully.

"Especially if we do it right," Lex added. "Dibs on chainsaw."

"I'll have to talk to Dad about borrowing his again," Adam reminded him.

"I'll get an apron and a burlap sack for a mask. It'll be awesome," Lex said with a grin.

"So, we have a chainsaw-toting madman. Anything else?" Adam looked at each of them in turn.

"Skeleton cowboy." Walter threw his hand up in the air.

"Same as last year?" Ken asked.

"And the year before?" Damien added.

Walter shrugged. "I like the coat and the hat. Keeps me warm, and I look badass."

Adam gave Walter a warning look and chided, "Mind the swearing, would you?" He jerked his head in his mother's direction.

Walter's eyes went wide. "Whoops, sorry. Forgot."

"Pretty sure your mouth works faster than your brain," Ken teased.

"Pretty sure there's not much that works faster than his mouth," Damien added.

Walter sighed, throwing his hands up in exasperation. "Is it not enough to be sorry?"

Lex laughed. "Nope. You should know that by now."

"Any slips of brain or tongue will be mocked without mercy," Adam stated matter-of-factly.

"Why is it always me who gets the mocking, though?" Walter whined, and all four of his friends looked at him simultaneously. He rolled his eyes and slumped his shoulders. "Point taken."

"Anyways, back to business. What about you, Damien?" Adam asked.

"Well...I kinda have this idea for a faceless demon. I'm gonna need chains and some Tripp pants...and maybe a set of glowing eyes..."

"Gonna try to make Red Eyes happen?" Walter asked, excitement in his voice.

Damien grinned mischievously. "Yeah, I think I got a way to do it finally." He had had the idea for a character he had dubbed "Red Eyes" for years now but had never elaborated on it before.

Adam grinned in turn. "Sounds awesome. As for me...mine will be a surprise."

Ken rolled his eyes. "Ever the showman."

Lex chuckled and asked, "Is there a reason you aren't part of the drama club at school?"

"Horror isn't on their selection list," Adam said with a shrug.

"Comedy's not too far from horror, you know," Damien argued.

Adam sighed. "Maybe next year I'll try it." He had almost forgotten that he hadn't told them about trying out for the fall play mere weeks ago, though he hadn't gotten a part. Pushing the memory to the back of his mind, he continued, "I prefer scaring anyways."

"You always have," Lex said.

"This year's gonna be great! I'm gonna make somebody pee themselves!" Walter declared excitedly.

"Any bets on who it will be?" Damien joked.

"If I had money, I'd put it on Kelsey," Ken suggested.

"That's obvious, though. She always overreacts," Adam said.

"Why else do we invite her?" Damien laughed.

"Fair enough." Assembling the guest list was always tricky business, so Adam decided to bring it up. "That reminds me, any suggestions for who else to invite?"

He was suddenly bombarded by a barrage of names from all directions. Adam held up his hands.

"Okay, okay! I didn't expect *that* much of a response!"

Ken blinked and shook his head in surprise. "You think we don't have friends?"

"Well...we are kinda the nerd herd," Adam admitted, embarrassed.

"Shamelessly!" Walter declared with a flip of his wild hair.

"Try talking to people, Adam. You might make some friends of your own," Damien teased.

Adam shrugged again. "I don't need to, really. I have you guys."

Silence hung in the air for a moment. Adam's face warmed a little.

Finally, Damien rolled his eyes. "Come on, man. Don't go getting all sappy on us."

"Yeah, no chick-flick moments," Ken concurred with a wave of his hand.

Adam considered attempting to defend himself but decided against it. Instead, he shook his head and got the conversation back on track. "Still, why don't we do it like this? You guys make your own guest lists and get them to me. I'll get a headcount and send out invitations. Sound fair?" There was a general murmur of agreement from the gang, so Adam nodded. "Cool. Now, don't we have a fight to finish?" he said with a sly smile.

At Adam's words, there was a mad rush for the living room from all but Ken. He simply followed the rest of his friends, laughing at their eagerness to continue the game.

LATER THAT NIGHT, THE boys lay about the living room, like they had a dozen times before. Damien claimed the couch, Ken sat under a blanket in the very same chair he'd occupied that afternoon, and the other three were in sleeping bags on the floor. However, sleep would be another few hours coming. They chatted about whatever came to mind.

Ken asked, "So, Adam, did you ask Taylor out yet?"

"It's only our first week of sophomore year. Give the man some time," Lex argued.

"He said he was going to ask her at the beginning of the school year, so I'm just asking if he did."

Adam's cheeks flushed, and he was glad the room was dark. With a sigh, he answered, "Yeah, but she turned me down."

"That's the pits, man," Walter consoled.

"Are you gonna try again?" Damien asked.

"Nah, I don't want to hound her." *Like she'd change her answer if I did.*

"Got your eyes on anyone else, then?" Walter glanced at Adam.

Damien scoffed. "You kidding? He's been crushing on Taylor since the fourth grade!"

"Yeah, only took me till now to actually ask her," Adam admitted.

"So, got your eye on anyone else yet?" Walter pressed.

Adam rolled his eyes, but his friend meant well. "Not at the moment. Kinda resigned to the single life."

"No need to be so negative," Lex interjected.

"Yeah! We're all just as big of nerds as you, and we've all had girlfriends!" Walter added.

Damien snorted. "Really? How many girlfriends have *you* had?"

"Enough," Walter answered cryptically.

"Your hand doesn't count," added Ken.

There was a snicker from the gang, along with an indignant huff from Walter, but then he finally admitted, "Just two."

"Only two? I've had like...five!" Damien retorted. "What about you, Lex?"

"Just a couple."

Adam remained silent. His answer had been the same all throughout his life.

Finally, Damien asked Ken, "How many for you again?"

"Fourteen."

"Jesus Christ!" Walter gasped.

"Lucky bastard," Damien grunted.

"Don't call it lucky. It means I fucked up fourteen times, so I'm single now."

Adam snorted. "Now who's being negative?"

"Still you," Ken countered. "You just have a confidence issue. You always have."

"I guess." But Adam was sure it was more reputation than anything else. He had grown up in Corbanton alongside most of his classmates, and they all remembered his awkward younger years, when he was the "weird kid." Reputations didn't die in Corbanton. Adam was certain that if he was going to ever have a chance at a relationship, it would have to be with a girl from outside Corbanton High School.

With a sigh, he rolled over in his sleeping bag and let himself drift off while his friends continued their banter.

2. New Girl Blues

Cassie stared out the rain-streaked car window. Her first day at Corbanton High School was not starting off well. Due to the downpour, Darcy had insisted Cassie be driven to school instead of walking. Naturally, Kaleb volunteered at once, much to Cassie's chagrin. She had kept her hate for him well hidden over the past three years, but his inability to see what was wrong with himself always tested her self-control. He never missed a chance for them to be alone together, and Cassie loathed him for it. However, she bit her tongue each time and settled for making her misery in his presence obvious.

Hoping he wouldn't try to make conversation on the way, Cassie rested her chin on her palm and sulkily watched the small houses of Corbanton. Her long, black hair served well to hide him from her view, especially with her hood up. Simply looking at him was nauseating. His smile made her skin crawl, and his casual tones in addressing her made her blood boil.

"So...," Kaleb began.

Fucking hell. "Don't," Cassie said curtly.

Blissful silence hung between them before he tried again. "You know..."

"Just shut up," she snapped without turning toward him. *How dare you act like you aren't a fucking monster.*

Kaleb heaved a sigh. "Moving here was not a good idea."

Cassie rolled her eyes. *This again.* "Drop it."

"Why did you want to move back here anyways?"

"You *know* who wanted us to move back here because it sure as fuck wasn't me," Cassie spat. Every second in conversation with him was excruciating. She snuck a glance at Kaleb to see if her reply had the desired effect. His eye twitched, and Cassie smirked. He always tried to pretend Asmodeous didn't exist, but Cassie loved how he squirmed when she reminded him.

Kaleb's voice rose an octave as he tried to continue the conversation. "Do you have any idea how difficult it was to convince your mother to go along with this?"

Cassie turned to look at him fully, her eyes blazing with malice. "Do you have any idea how hard it was for *him* to convince me not to kill you?"

"You wouldn't dare!" Kaleb gasped, his eyes nearly bulging and a vein in his temple pulsing visibly.

"That would be true if you hadn't tried to rape me!"

Kaleb winced, and his voice fell to almost a whisper. "Stop bringing that up."

"Then stop fucking talking to me," Cassie snapped before turning away once more. Her point must have gotten across since he didn't try to make conversation again until they were pulling up to the front entrance of the high school.

Corbanton High was a single-story building of brick and mortar, stretching far in both directions. This did little to lighten Cassie's mood. With everything on one floor level, all of her classes would undoubtedly be spread out. She heaved a sigh and thought, *I hope you know what you're doing.*

Fear not, said the soft, dry voice.

All right, I'm trusting you on this. It better be worth it. Not expecting Asmodeous to answer, Cassie opened the car door and stepped out, book bag in hand.

"Have a good day!" Kaleb called with an awkwardly high-pitched voice.

Drop dead. Cassie kept her thoughts to herself as she slammed the car door. To a passerby, Kaleb would have sounded cheerful, but Cassie knew his uncomfortable voice all too well. The most sickening part of that man was his ability to put on a front of normalcy whenever there was any risk of someone hearing or seeing them. Cassie went along with it for Asmodeous's purposes, but every time it happened, she wanted to vomit. With a sigh, she set off up the sidewalk and opened the school's glass front door.

The contrast between the gloomy outside and the brightly lit interior of the school was nearly blinding at first. The walls and ceiling were bare, the monotony broken only by a handful of pictures showing honor roll students and the administrative staff. Black sectional couches sat against the walls on both sides of the entryway. Most were occupied by groups of students hanging out before classes began. A few of them turned to look in Cassie's direction. They seemed curious, nothing more. *Understandable.*

Cassie imagined how she must appear to them. She was average height for a girl of sixteen and completely covered by baggy black pants and a hooded sweatshirt to match. Only her hands, face, and a few strands of hair were visible. The past three years had been filled with getting the wrong sort of attention for how she dressed, and so now she was in a new place, Cassie was taking great pains to not stand out. She had hoped no one would notice her on her way to the office, but her annoyance grew as more and more heads turned in her direction.

Great.

Cassie was relieved when the office door closed, shielding "the new girl" from staring eyes. She pulled down her hood and smoothed her hair before turning toward the reception desk. The woman behind it had short, wavy black hair that reminded Cassie of a storm cloud. She looked slightly past middle-aged, with light wrinkles around her eyes and mouth. A pair of half-moon spectacles rested on her nose, and she typed away on a keyboard Cassie couldn't see over the front of the desk.

"Excuse me?" Cassie inquired politely.

The receptionist stopped typing and looked up at her with a raised eyebrow. "Can I help you?"

Cassie bristled. *So that's how it's gonna be?* "It's my first day here. Cassandra Ebonwood."

The receptionist nodded. "Right, right." She dipped out of sight behind the desk. Papers ruffled about before she re-emerged with a navy-blue folder and handed it to Cassie. Her name was on the front in permanent marker. "This has your class schedule, a school map, your locker number and combination, and a refresher on our policies. Your parents did go over them with you beforehand, correct?" she asked, her expression severe.

My parents are dead. The words almost spilled out of Cassie's mouth in her rising annoyance with the receptionist's attitude, but she had learned nothing if not self-control over the past three years. "Yes, they did," she lied. Darcy's work as a real estate agent was picking up with the seasons changing from summer to fall, and Cassie would rather drive her prized cross-hilted dagger into Kaleb's throat than sit down to go over anything with him. School policies were hardly unique things anyway.

The receptionist seemed satisfied, however. "Very good, then. Will you need a guide to find your first class?"

"I can manage, thank you," Cassie said as sweetly as she could, despite her irritation. *What kind of idiot do you take me for? You gave me a fucking map!*

Calm yourself, Asmodeous warned, his words echoing in her mind.

Cassie took a deep breath. *I know, I know. She's just annoying.*

As though to emphasize Cassie's thoughts, the receptionist, another eyebrow raised, asked, "Will there be anything else, then?"

Not if I can help it. "No, I'm good. Thank you." Cassie opened the folder and pulled out the map to find her first class. As she left the office, she focused intensely on the room numbers, hoping to block out the curious stares. Still, whether she imagined it or not, she could feel their eyes on her. What were they thinking about? She tried not to wonder, but not knowing put her on edge. Monsters like Kaleb were everywhere.

Cassie breathed a sigh of relief when she found the room for her first class. It was a short distance from the entryway, nestled in a spot all its own with no neighboring classrooms. Cassie went inside and had to do a double take as she looked around. Almost every inch of the walls that wasn't markerboard or door was covered by a poster of a book-to-film adaptation. Cassie even recognized a good number of them. *What kind of class is this?* She checked her schedule again to be sure, but there it was in black and white: *English 10, Mr. Martinez.*

Cassie checked the markerboard behind the small teacher's desk at the front of the room, but it was blank. She assumed she could sit wherever and picked a desk in the back corner before taking another quizzical look around.

A tall, bearded man walked in. His hair was thinning and peppered with spots of gray and white, and his beady, light-blue eyes peered out from behind a pair of wireframe glasses. He was dressed in a scarlet turtleneck and khaki pants, and he carried a large binder under his arm.

That must be Mr. Martinez.

Mr. Martinez glanced around the room before his eyes settled on Cassie. "Oh, hello!" He had a deep, powerful voice despite his amicable tone.

Cassie's guard immediately went up. "Hi," she said with a friendly smile.

Mr. Martinez slid over to his desk and looked down at a paper. "Oh, so you must be Cassandra Ebonwood."

"Cassie, please."

"Cassie it is." He smiled up at her again as he seated himself behind his desk. "Well, welcome to Corbanton! How are you liking it so far?"

Cassie's smile faltered a little. "It's all right. It's really small."

Mr. Martinez nodded knowingly, folding his arms and leaning back in his chair. "It is, but it has its charms." However, their conversation was cut short when other students began trickling into the room. To Cassie's surprise, Mr. Martinez greeted them all heartily and by name, just as he had her.

Despite herself, her guard relaxed a bit. *Maybe he is just genuinely friendly.* As he spoke, she even found herself admiring the power in his voice. He seemed as though he could command a room with ease.

Cassie was proven right in her assessment of Mr. Martinez as class began. After the bell rang, he stood up and led a discussion on a chapter from a novel the students had been assigned to read over the weekend. He encouraged participation from everyone, including a very soft-spoken boy named Adam in the opposite back corner. Cassie found her admiration for Mr. Martinez growing. *If all the teachers are like this, things might not be so bad.*

Unfortunately, throughout the rest of the day, Cassie found that Mr. Martinez was the exception rather than the rule. As if it weren't enough that she was already familiar with the material being taught, the other teachers droned on and on with little engagement from their classes. Cassie's mind drifted throughout the day, and she snuck glances at the other students from the corners of her eyes. To her surprise, many of her classes were shared with the same students, something occurring only rarely in the city school she had gone to previously. Cassie appreciated the familiarity, though. *Time to see who's dangerous.*

By the day's end, Cassie's frustration was mounting. Most of the classes didn't offer time to assess who she was going to class with, and the instruction was unbearably dull. Still, when the bell rang for the end of the day, Cassie was relieved to see the skies had cleared from that morning's rain. Instead of the main entrance, she headed out the cafeteria doors. From there, it would be a quick walk across the bus-filled parking lot, across the street, and through a large patch of woods to her house.

The heat of the late afternoon sun during her trek and humidity from the morning rain had her soaked in sweat. Cassie yearned to free herself from the scorching confines of her baggy clothes but refrained from doing so. *No one can see.*

Careful to hide all signs of discomfort, even as she worked her way through the woods, Cassie plodded on until, at last, she was in front of her house. It was a small brick ranch, simple and quaint. Darcy had balked at buying such a small home, but Cassie had had no trouble using the threat of exposing Kaleb to convince him to talk Darcy into it. Even though it was small, it was lovely.

Much to Cassie's relief, only Darcy's car was in the driveway. She gratefully opened the door and stepped into the air conditioning. *Whatever the law firm has him doing, I hope it takes all night.*

The house's charm carried through the parlor and dining room and into a sunroom opposite the front door, where Darcy was working at a computer. "Welcome home! How was school?" Darcy asked without turning to face her.

Engrossed as always. Unable to contain her annoyance any longer, Cassie heaved a sigh. "Pretty damn boring."

"That's nice, dear," Darcy replied absently, continuing her work.

Cassie rolled her eyes and set off down the hall for her bedroom. When Darcy wasn't distracted with her work, she was busy living in a fantasy world where Kaleb could do no wrong. Whether the pretenses had her fooled or Darcy was just naïve, Cassie couldn't tell. Either way, she had grown to hate her adoptive mother almost as much as she hated Kaleb.

Once inside her room, Cassie closed the door and locked it before turning her ceiling fan up to the max. Her room was simple and unadorned, with only a dresser, her bed, and the standing mirror. *Alone at last.*

Still soaked with sweat, Cassie immediately stripped down to her underwear, savoring the cool air against her skin. As she crossed the room, however, she caught sight of herself in the mirror. Without the baggie clothes, Cassie's natural beauty was undeniable. Her skin was soft and smooth as silk, and her curves had only grown more alluring as she had aged. Tears filled her eyes. Cassie knew she was gorgeous...and she hated it.

Turning away from her reflection, Cassie threw herself on her bed and cried in silence. Her good looks had brought her nothing but trouble. Just as Asmodeous had said, as soon as she had begun to bloom into a young woman, people had started to look at her differently. No matter what she did, the words "whore" and "slut" followed her around whenever her figure was remotely visible. They echoed in her mind every time she took her clothes off, overwhelming her with the urge to cover herself. She had thought more girls would be sympathetic, but they were often among those who spread the most rumors. Was it jealousy? Cassie didn't care; she just wanted a friend.

Then there were the catcalls. Cassie's fingernails dug into her palms, recalling every time a guy had heckled her. *Despicable pigs.* She shook with barely contained rage at the half-dozen guys who had tried to corner and take advantage of her. Most had ended up in the hospital. She hated them all. Still, the worst were those like Kaleb: those who pretended to care about her, only for her to later find that they just wanted to sleep with her.

What Cassie hated most of all about her looks was how much she wanted to show them. She had never lost her love of feeling pretty or attractive, but the attention she got wasn't worth it. In fact, she preferred just to cover herself from head to toe rather than be stared at like a piece of meat or called a whore for having a sizeable chest. Time and again, she had been stabbed in the back over her looks, proving there was only one she could trust.

Heaving a miserable sigh, Cassie rolled over and stared up at the ceiling. Her tears dried beneath the fan's gentle breeze. *I hope you know what you're doing,* she thought for the second time that day.

Do not worry, Asmodeous answered. *All things in time.*

Cassie sighed again but did not argue. Asmodeous always counseled patience, and he had yet to steer her wrong. Whatever reason he had for needing them to move back to Corbanton must have been important. Given how he had looked after her for thirteen years, Cassie felt no need to ask him why.

All things in time, she repeated in her head, closing her eyes and listening to the soft hum of the ceiling fan.

3. Hesitant Curiosity

Adam joined his friends on the couches in the school entrance hallway. Ever since they had started high school, it had been their morning meet-up spot of choice. The topics of discussion were as varied as the personalities among them, but it came as no surprise when Damien said, "So...what do you guys make of the new girl?"

Lex was first to answer. "I'm not sure, honestly. She spent the entire day alone, not talking to anyone."

Adam shrugged. "She seemed like she wanted to be left alone." She had sat in the opposite back corner of his English class, which was usually a telltale sign of not wanting to stand out. Adam could empathize and had avoided making eye contact. English wasn't the only class they shared; however, their eyes had met only once. He'd never seen such a deep shade of blue. With her pale complexion and dark hair, her eyes seemed to shine even brighter, and that brief moment of meeting them might have lasted an eternity if the bell hadn't rung.

His cheeks suddenly felt warm.

Thankfully, Walter pulled all attention away from Adam. "Gotta say, though, her face is pretty easy on the eyes."

His words met with a general murmur of agreement from the group. Then Ken added, "Makes you wonder what the rest of her looks like."

Adam stiffened slightly. It wasn't hard to see where the conversation was about to go, but it didn't make him any less uncomfortable.

Damien shrugged. "It can't be anything special if she's covering it all up like she is."

Maybe she just doesn't want a bunch of perverts drooling over it. Adam appreciated a pretty girl as much as any guy, but how forward Ken and Damien could be about sexualizing girls bugged him.

The warning bell for first class sounded, and Adam was relieved to have an excuse to abandon the conversation before speculation could continue.

After a brief farewell, Adam headed down the hall to Mr. Martinez's room. To his surprise, the new girl was already there—he hadn't seen her walk through the front doors that morning. Adam quickly averted his eyes and made for his seat in the opposite corner. With any luck, she hadn't noticed his shock at seeing her. *Will she think I've been watching her or something?* His chest tightened in fear. *What if she thinks I'm some kind of creep?*

Blinking, Adam mentally chastised himself. Why should he be worried about what the new girl thought of him? The odds weren't in his favor of them ever having a conversation anyway.

Students came into the classroom in groups, but no one greeted the new girl, and she greeted no one in turn. Had she not made any friends? Did she even care about making friends? Was she just shy?

Adam was careful to keep his eyes forward throughout the class. Still, he couldn't deny his curiosity about the new girl. What was her name? Where had she come from? He could just see her out of the corner of his eye as Mr. Martinez led another discussion on Dante's *Inferno*. The new girl seemed as interested in the discussion as Adam himself had been before the unexpected distraction. With a quiet sigh, he forced his attention back to Mr. Martinez. It was pointless to dwell on any questions about the new girl. *Odds are we'll never speak to each other anyways.*

Unfortunately, questions about the new girl ran through his mind throughout the day, and his thoughts continued to linger on her when he and his friends sat at their usual table at lunch.

"Well, her name's Cassie," Ken said as they all leaned into the table conspiratorially—all except for Adam.

"She finally said something to someone?" Damien asked.

"The teacher called on her in U.S. history," Ken explained, though his expression was puzzled.

"And...?" Walter asked, leaning forward eagerly.

"Well...honestly, she's really smart. I can't even remember what the teacher asked her about, but she gave a...well...a pretty impressive answer. The teacher didn't know what to say."

Adam perked up immediately. Next to English, history classes were among his favorites, but then he remembered who they were talking about. *You don't have a chance, so forget it.*

"Intimidated by a girl with a brain?" Walter joked.

"You weren't there," Ken countered.

Adam frowned. Something about Cassie's answer to the teacher's question seemed to have troubled Ken. "What were you guys talking about?"

Ken shrugged. "Life in the early U.S., after the Revolutionary War and everything."

"And she shocked the teacher into silence?" Lex asked.

Ken nodded. "She sounded like she was reading aloud from a textbook. She didn't even have hers open."

"Did he call on her again?" asked Walter.

Ken shook his head. "I think it rattled him."

Damien folded his arms and leaned back in his chair. "Sounds like she might be a bit of a weirdo."

Adam bristled. "Because she's a U.S. history buff?"

"I dunno, man," Ken interjected. "It is prolly best if she's just left alone."

"Maybe that's why she gave her answer the way she did," added Lex.

Adam frowned. *Maybe indeed.*

Throughout the remainder of the day, what little information Adam had picked up about Cassie only stoked his curiosity about her. Was she a history buff? What other subjects might she be interested in? It seemed like she was into *Inferno* as well. Perhaps they might find they had a lot in common, especially if she was shy. For a moment, Adam considered trying to talk to her, but then he remembered himself. *You're the class nerd. Just forget about it.*

Adam's curiosity dogged him all the way until the end of the day. As he stepped out of the cafeteria doors to the parking lot where the school buses lined up, he saw a familiar profile looking both ways and crossing the street with her back to him. Caught off guard, Adam watched Cassie walk across the street and into the woods on the other side. *Bet she lives on the other side of the woods.* That would explain why she hadn't come in the main entrance that morning. Again, as always, she was alone.

Adam watched Cassie disappear into the trees and felt sympathetic toward her. Despite having grown up in Corbanton, he still knew how it felt to be an outsider. He and his friends had banded together from among the students in their grade as a group of social outcasts with similar interests.

With Cassie lost to view, Adam headed toward his bus. What if she isolated herself for the same reason he and his friends did? What if they were the type of friends she needed?

Adam boarded the bus, passing the seats occupied by the middle schoolers up front to the middle, where a handful of elementary students sat. Among them was Adam's eight-year-old cousin, Evey Malroy. The rear of the bus was reserved for the high schoolers, but Adam preferred the company of his cousin. He found her sitting in a seat alone, as usual, kicking her legs aimlessly and staring off into space. She had short, dark hair, and her bangs were pinned back by a pink-flowered barrette. Evey was small and slender, wearing a white blouse with blue jean overalls and colorful tennis shoes. She would have passed for a normal eight-year-old if not for the noise-cancelling earmuffs she wore.

Adam sat down beside her and slowly waved a hand in front of her face to get her attention. Evey turned, her face splitting into a bright grin as she pulled off the earmuffs. "Hi, A. K.!" she tittered cheerfully. Evey always referred to him as A. K. for his first and middle name.

"Hello, Evey," Adam greeted her in turn with a smile. "How was school today?"

"Pretty boring," Evey replied with a frown. "Mrs. Mummert made me go over the same thing we did…"

As Evey rambled about her classes, Adam listened quietly, though only half paying attention. His cousin was extremely troubled. He couldn't recall the exact disorders she had, but she was medicated heavily. On top of all of that, she had to keep her art supplies and earmuffs around at all times. Too much noise would send her into a bizarre sort of fit which would have her drawing furiously. If Evey didn't have her materials at hand when such a fit came on, she would panic and try to improvise, regardless of hurting herself in the process or not.

Adam recalled the lesson he had learned from what had happened to his cousin. Nobody talked about Aunt Priscilla or why she had hidden herself and Evey away from the family, but one day, Evey had ended up with their grandmother. What had led to that was a secret only a handful of people knew, and Adam wasn't among them. Still, the entire incident had taught him to respect the fact he could never truly understand what was going on in someone's private life, let alone how they dealt with it.

This brought his thoughts back to Cassie. Who knew why she kept to herself? She could be troubled, just like Evey, or maybe she preferred the quiet and solitude simply because. Adam certainly found moments when he was overwhelmed by too many people around him at once, even among his friends. Still, he could only guess, and despite himself, his curiosity dogged him, even as he bade farewell to Evey getting off of the bus at their grandmother's house, and then as he got off at his own house just a few minutes later.

The rest of the week passed much the same as that Tuesday. Adam constantly lost focus in every class he shared with Cassie, though he tried to work up the courage to talk to her. She remained alone and unbothered, her expression unreadable. No teachers called on her to answer any questions, and Adam never saw anyone approach her. His friends didn't bring her up again since no new information had surfaced after Ken's experience with her in U.S. history.

The hardest for Adam was at the end of each day, however. He would almost always catch Cassie in the process of crossing the parking lot or the street before disappearing into the woods. Each time, he considered trying to catch up to her and start a conversation, but his courage always failed. Surely, she had no interest in talking to a nerd like him. Few girls did.

On Friday, Adam emerged from the school to find Cassie making her usual walk. Resigning himself to his inability to approach her, Adam headed for his bus parked at the back of the line. As he rounded the last bus before his, he caught a glimpse of something peculiar at the tree line. Several yards down from where Cassie usually entered the woods, a group of five large students he recognized as football players congregated. *What are they up to?*

The five of them glanced around before heading into the woods. Curious, Adam tried to guess what direction they were going. He still had no idea of their intent until he remembered stories he had heard for years. Though the woods were well within the town limits, there was no more secluded place in the entirety of Corbanton. Stories circulated regularly of numerous teens taking advantage of that to do drugs or have sex.

Then Adam's stomach turned over: the jocks' trajectory would lead them directly toward where Cassie had gone.

Adam's heart raced. Was that what they were intending to do? He didn't like the sly expressions on their faces, nor the way they looked around conspiratorially before going in after her. The thought of what five guys of their size might do to one girl alone made Adam want to vomit.

He froze. Could he even make it in time? What if he did? Could he do anything to stop them?

I have to do something! I have to warn her!

Adam threw caution to the wind, dashing across the street and into the woods after Cassie. He ran as fast as his legs could carry him, ducking branches and dodging roots in his race to reach her before the jocks did. When he found her, relief washed over him; the jock gang was nowhere in sight. He raced up to her side and tried to speak but was gasping for breath.

Cassie whirled around and crouched into a defensive stance, her hands raised and balled into fists. "Who are you? What do you want?" she snapped, her eyes wide and suspicious.

"Five...five guys...," Adam wheezed.

Cassie cocked her head. "Excuse me?"

Adam finally started catching his breath. "There...five football...players. Came in...after you. Run!"

Cassie blinked in surprise. "You're...warning me?"

Adam nodded earnestly and urged, "Run! Now!"

Cassie looked taken aback, but she lowered her hands and relaxed her stance. "Wow. That's...actually really sweet of you."

Adam lost himself for a moment. Of all the reactions he had expected, that wasn't one of them. For a moment, his head was blank, and all he could see was her face, with those lustrous blue eyes looking at him—how smooth her cheeks and forehead were, and how...

Adam blinked and remembered why he had caught up with her in the first place. "They're coming after you! Haven't you heard what happens in these woods?"

"Well...not really, but I can look after myself, believe me," Cassie assured him.

"You don't understand. These guys are..."

"I'm sorry, what was that?" a voice called from behind Adam.

His back stiffened, and his eyes widened in horror. The next moment, two of the jocks grabbed Adam by the arms and dragged him away from Cassie. One was a bulky, blond-haired boy named Dustin and the other an imposing redhead named Greg. A third grabbed Cassie and pinned her against a tree by the throat. The last two looked around as if making sure they weren't being watched.

Cassie made no move to struggle, her expression betraying only mild surprise. The guy who had her pinned was lanky but muscled, with a dark flat-top haircut and brown eyes. Adam recognized him as Ian Drake, the football captain.

Ian looked around and asked, "Is the coast clear?"

"We're all alone here," a deep voice answered from behind Adam, and the last two stepped into view.

One was a husky blond named Chris, the other a dark-haired brute named Quinn. They flanked Ian, glancing around once again to confirm their report.

"Good," Ian said with a satisfied smirk before turning to look at Cassie. "Nobody turns me down, bitch," he growled.

He must've hit on her and gotten the cold shoulder.

Cassie didn't respond, but her eyes looked unblinkingly back into his.

How the hell is she so calm?

"Not so tough now, are you?" Ian jeered.

Once again, Cassie remained silent. Adam had to admire her nerve; she showed no outward sign of fear, even as Ian held her pinned by her throat still.

He hissed at her, "Makes a guy wonder what you're so eager to hide under those baggy clothes of yours."

Could this get any worse? Adam's stomach was doing cartwheels. He should try screaming for help, but they'd be on him in seconds. There had to be something he could do, but it wasn't coming to him.

The jocks circled Cassie like vultures.

"Wonder how many you've let see what's under there," Ian pondered aloud, looking Cassie's body up and down eagerly.

Adam swore he was about to throw up. Still, Cassie seemed unphased.

As if goaded by her silence, Ian sneered. "I bet you're a talented little slut. Bet you can handle five cocks at once, no problem."

Still, Cassie said nothing.

Ian's eye twitched for a moment before he called to his companions, "What do you think, guys? Want to find out how loud this whore can scream?"

"What about peewee here?" Dustin asked, lifting Adam by his arm for a moment.

Adam winced but made no sound. If Cassie could face them calmly and silently, he could too.

"He can watch. It'll prolly be the closest he'll ever get to a naked woman," Ian said, not looking away from Cassie.

His companions guffawed maliciously.

"I call dibs on fucking her ass!" Dustin tightened his grip on Adam's arm.

"You can do that while I fuck her throat," Quinn added.

"Let's see how big her tits are!" Greg nearly trembled with anticipation.

Ian smirked as he hissed, "We're gonna fill all your holes, you fucking slut. By the time we're done with you, you won't be able to walk for a month."

Adam's throat burned. Panic threatened to overwhelm him.

What Cassie said next silenced them all immediately.

"Choke me harder."

Ian blinked in surprise, then narrowed his eyes. "What did you just say?"

Cassie closed her eyes for a moment, letting the quiet hang in the air. All five guys stared in confusion. When she opened her eyes again, they were blazing.

"I said, 'choke me *harder*.'"

Nothing could have prepared Adam for what happened next. Cassie's knee shot up into her captor's groin. Ian released her and clutched at his crotch, falling to his knees. Before he even hit the ground, Cassie spun on the spot, punching Ian in the temple. He twisted in turn and crumbled to the ground in a silent heap.

"What the...," Greg gasped.

Everyone was too shocked to move—except for Cassie. In the seconds of stunned stillness after Ian fell, she had already whirled around to kick Chris in the gut, knocking the breath from his lungs. When he doubled over, Cassie spun in a roundhouse kick to the side of his head. Like Ian before him, Chris went down silently.

Quinn finally snapped out of his stupor and lunged at Cassie with his hands outstretched. Without looking at him, she bobbed aside and threw her elbow back, smashing into his face. There was an audible crack, and Quinn grunted in pain, blood spraying down his face. He stumbled, still caught in the momentum of his lunge as he fell to the ground.

Dustin released Adam and dove low to catch Cassie by the midsection. Once again, she seemed to anticipate the maneuver and rolled into a leap over him, slamming her knee into his back. Dustin gasped in pain, his arms flying outward, and he belly-flopped to the ground. She rose swiftly back into her stance and looked around for any more attackers.

Greg stepped behind Adam, grabbing both of his arms as if to use him as a human shield. "Stay back, or I'll snap him in half!" Greg warned, his voice suddenly an octave higher than normal. His grip on Adam trembled for a completely different reason than it had mere moments ago.

Cassie turned to face them, her eyes narrow and cold. Dustin was trying to rise from where she had knocked him to the ground, but Cassie planted one foot on his back and forced him down without taking her eyes off of Greg. She smirked. "Now who's afraid?"

Greg barked, "Just stay back, or Romeo gets it!"

He squeezed Adam's arms painfully, but Adam barely noticed. His mind was still trying to process what he had just witnessed.

Once again, Dustin tried to rise. Cassie sighed, rolling her eyes before launching a vicious kick into his ribs. He rolled over, gasping and coughing and clutching at his side. With a satisfied smirk, Cassie turned her eyes back on Greg, but he dragged Adam a step back.

Cassie's gaze then shifted to something over Greg's shoulder and widened. She pointed and shouted, "Look out behind you!"

Adam didn't fall for the trick, but Greg was not so quick-witted. Greg gasped, and his grip slacked on Adam's arms. The next instant, Cassie was beside them, pushing Adam aside as she delivered blow after blow to Greg. Adam stumbled, and by the time he found his feet again, Greg, too, was on the ground in a heap.

Adam looked around at the carnage: Quinn was rolling on the ground with his hands over his shattered nose; Dustin was in the fetal position, clutching his ribs; and Ian, Chris, and Greg were all unconscious. Despite himself, he stared as Cassie flipped her long hair and adjusted her baggy clothes, her breathing astoundingly steady and controlled.

She turned to look at Adam and grinned. "See? I told you I can take care of myself!"

4. The First Step

Silence hung in the air between them as both Cassie and the boy from her classes—Adam—surveyed the scene. Adam was stunned, but Cassie was satisfied. Sure, her skills were formidable. She had stuck to her training since the day after the incident with Kaleb. Still, even she shouldn't have been able to take down five football players by herself...without a little help.

Asmodeous had informed her of every upcoming move, guiding her to dodge one attack, then the next, until she was in control of the situation. But nothing had been as satisfying as seeing the mindless terror in the eyes of the creep who had been holding Adam. There *had* been something over his shoulder when Cassie had called to him, but before he could even begin to make out Asmodeous's shape, Cassie had laid him out.

Say something to him, Asmodeous whispered. He had returned to her shadow, probably to avoid Adam's attention.

Cassie gave a start of surprise, but Adam didn't seem to notice. Not questioning Asmodeous, she said the first thing she could think of. "Well...I still think it was sweet of you to warn me. It's possible they could have gotten the better of me if you hadn't gotten here first."

Adam stuttered, "How...How did you..."

Cassie shrugged. "I like to fight."

"I...I see that," Adam observed, looking around at the crumpled bodies on the ground. Once again, silence hung between them.

Ask to see him here tomorrow.

Cassie's eyes widened. *What? Why?*

Trust me.

"Are you busy tomorrow?" Cassie blurted out. It was pretty convenient that tomorrow was Saturday.

Adam's head snapped back to her, his brow furrowed in disbelief. "Uh...I don't think so?"

"Why...Why don't you meet me at the edge of the woods tomorrow?" she asked, trying to sound surer of herself than she felt. *I really hope you know what you're doing, Master.*

Adam blinked in surprise. "You mean...You mean you want to hang out? With me?"

Cassie was taken aback. He seemed as confused as she was. Trying to make light of the awkward situation, she gave a half-smile and tried to sound playful. "Well, duh! I asked you to, didn't I?"

Adam's mouth opened and closed several times, like a fish with his eyes wide. When the image popped into her head, Cassie couldn't suppress a giggle.

Adam's cheeks flushed, and he mumbled, "Well...yeah, but...this is the last thing I expected."

The giggle eased the tension of the situation, and Cassie found her reply coming naturally. "Was that before or after what you just saw?"

"Either," Adam answered with a shrug. "I just couldn't stand there and do nothing about...you know...*them.*" He gestured toward the fallen jock gang.

Awfully brave of you. "It really *was* sweet of you to do that. You kinda earned this, don't you think?" Being playful with him was actually sort of fun for her.

"If...If you say so," he stammered, clearly still in shock.

"I'm Cassie. Cassie Ebonwood." She extended her hand.

"Adam Sullivan."

They shook hands in greeting. His grip was firm but surprisingly gentle for a teenage boy.

"We have a few classes together, don't we?"

Adam's cheeks turned pink, and Cassie giggled again. It was weirdly cute.

"I...I guess so."

"Well, nice to actually meet you, then. So will I be seeing you here tomorrow?" Cassie asked brightly.

"I think so," Adam answered meekly, but then his eyes widened. He glanced back the way he had come. "I...I gotta call a friend. I missed the bus..."

Cassie couldn't hide her surprise. "Just to warn me?"

Adam turned back to face her, but his cheeks had gone from pink to red.

How noble of him. "I look forward to getting to know you a little better tomorrow, then," she said with a smile that almost felt genuine.

Almost.

Adam offered a shy smile in return. "Me too. What time?"

In the morning.

Following Asmodeous's word, Cassie suggested, "How about ten o'clock?"

Adam nodded. "That'll work. See you then?"

Cassie gave another smile and waved. "See you then!"

Adam turned around and headed back the way he had come, pulling his phone from his pocket.

Maybe she was a little impressed by his bravery, but no one could protect her like Asmodeous. Still, his request puzzled her. *What was that all about?*

That boy...he will do quite nicely.

Then, Cassie understood. *I think you're right.*

We should deal with the others, however. Best that they do not repeat anything they witnessed here.

Cassie looked around at the crumpled and groaning bodies of the jock gang. *How should we do it?* An image popped into Cassie's mind of her demanding Ian's silence as she stomped on his crotch. She giggled aloud at the thought of his eyes popping out in pain.

Apparently, Asmodeous had other plans. *I shall handle it.*

Aww, damn. Still, Cassie didn't argue. Then before her eyes, five dark tendrils extended from her shadow. They slithered along the ground until they each reached one of the jocks. A couple were stirring, and one was even starting to look around.

As the tendril slithered toward him, he rolled over and tried to back away on his elbows. "What is that? Get it away!"

"Shhhh, it'll all be over soon," Cassie whispered, delighted by his terror.

The shadows then lifted themselves off the ground and pressed to each of the jocks' foreheads. The one fully conscious had a moment to scream in fear before the touch of the tendril rendered him unconscious. All five were then silent and still.

How much will they remember?

They will remember assembling at the edge of the woods and nothing more until they awaken.

Best I make myself scarce, then. Without further ado, Cassie set off for home. However, much to her dismay, Kaleb's car was in the driveway when she emerged from the woods. Worse still, Darcy's was not. *Great.*

You will need permission to go through with tomorrow.

From him, though? Cassie shuddered with disgust.

Remember your leverage.

Cassie's lips turned upward in a subtle smile. *With pleasure.* With renewed determination, Cassie crossed the street and entered the house.

Kaleb was waiting in a chair in the front parlor. "How was school today?" he asked cheerfully.

"I'm going out tomorrow. I won't be home most of the day," Cassie stated firmly.

"Excuse me?" Kaleb frowned.

"You heard me."

"Are you planning on telling me where?"

"Would you also like me to tell Darcy about you sneaking into my bedroom three years ago?"

Kaleb blanched. "You...Why do you have to keep bringing that up? It was just a one-time thing!"

Cassie snorted. "I'd believe that if you were a little quieter when you jacked off outside my bedroom door the other night."

Kaleb fell silent, his eyes wide. Cassie almost laughed at how pathetic he was.

"What...What should I tell your mom, then?" he stammered.

Cassie headed toward the hallway, waving her hand dismissively. "Make something up, but if it's not convincing enough *or* causes her to give me any trouble, she'll be the first to find out what you really are, followed by the cops."

Kaleb said nothing in reply, and as Cassie got closer to her bedroom, her face lit up with savage triumph. *Serves him right.*

Cassie slipped away to her room and locked the door as usual. For a moment, she stood with her back to it, almost giddy at how the day was turning out. However, though Asmodeous had taught her breathing techniques so she wouldn't get winded during a fight, nothing could stop the stream of sweat pouring out of her from moving so much under baggy clothes. She turned the ceiling fan on full blast and shed her clothes entirely to cool off.

As Cassie sat on the edge of the bed, letting the fan dry her off, her thoughts turned to the next stage of the plan. Ever since they had moved to Corbanton, Asmodeous had told her to keep an eye out for a suitable candidate. Now that they had chosen one, the next stage fell solely to her. Cassie was nervous, even hesitant, about what she would have to do, but she trusted Asmodeous completely. He wouldn't lead her into something she couldn't handle.

Still... Cassie slid off the bed and stood in front of her mirror once again, looking herself up and down. As usual, she felt uncomfortable and even ashamed of what she was looking at. The next step would involve getting close to Adam...and Cassie wasn't ready for it. She could almost see Kaleb's eyes looking back at her from Adam's face, and a chill ran down her spine.

Trust in me, Asmodeous whispered. *The boy will be no threat to you.*

"I hope you're right." Asmodeous seemed confident, but Cassie was nervous. Adam had seemed meek enough, but without fail, men always changed the more they saw of her.

Use it against him.

Cassie blinked. *How...?*

You are stronger than him.

She looked at herself in the mirror once again. However, instead of fixating on her curves or her sizeable chest, Cassie noticed the tone of her muscles. She *was* stronger than him...easily. If Adam tried anything, she could break him, just like one of the five jocks. Cassie was in control, and one way or another, the next step would proceed on her terms.

Her lips curled into a confident smile. *He's as good as ours.*

5. Alone in the Woods

Adam reached the edge of the woods and found Ken's black car in the cafeteria parking lot, waiting for him. After checking that the coast was clear, Adam crossed the street and climbed in.

Ken threw the gearshift into drive. "So, what made Mr. Punctuality miss the bus today?"

Adam flushed a little, trying to think of what to say. He was still stunned by what had happened mere minutes ago, leaving him unsure how to tell the tale. Ultimately, he decided on the truth and relayed to Ken the entirety of what happened—from the moment he saw Cassie at the edge of the woods to when he climbed into Ken's car.

When Adam's story was done, Ken didn't respond right away. He frowned for a moment, then laughed.

Adam's face burned. "What's so funny?"

Ken stifled his chuckle. "I don't think you can handle her."

"After what I just saw, I don't think anyone can." Adam stared out the windshield.

Ken shrugged. "You may be right about that." There was silence for a moment before his expression turned serious. "You may want to be careful with her, though."

Adam turned to face Ken with a frown. "Why?"

"She's smart, she can kick some serious ass, and she doesn't talk to anyone."

"I don't talk to other people much either."

"You talk to me and the guys," Ken countered.

"True, but we've known each other for ten years, at least."

"All the same, be careful with her. She may genuinely like you, or she may have an ulterior motive. Just don't let your guard down," Ken warned.

Adam sighed. "I mean...I guess you're right." He hated to admit it, but the likelihood of a girl like Cassie taking a shine to him out of the blue was pretty farfetched. Ken had a habit of telling harsh truths, but his advice was always in his friends' best interest.

"I don't want to rain on your parade. She's pretty cute and wants to hang out with you. You can and should enjoy it. Just don't get too attached too quickly, all right?" Ken advised.

"I'll try. By the way...when we get done hanging out tomorrow, will you give me a ride home? I'd kinda like to not let my parents know about her yet."

Ken laughed. "Sneaking around already?"

"Mom will gush and ask questions, and Dad will just ask questions," Adam replied.

Ken bobbed his head in agreement. "Fair enough. As far as they'll know, you were with me the whole time."

"Thanks a lot," Adam said gratefully as they turned onto his driveway. It wound up a hill for about a quarter of a mile before opening into a small gravel parking area where both of his parents' vehicles sat. The garage was attached to a two-story country house with a wrap-around covered porch and faded yellow siding. The porch railing and supports were painted green, with flecks of paint peeling off, revealing brown underneath.

Ken pulled up in front of the other parked cars and Adam got out. "Thanks again, man."

"Anytime," Ken replied cheerfully.

Adam closed the car door, made his way through the garage, and then stepped into the laundry room, all while pondering what he was going to tell his mother about Saturday. He paused in the laundry room before closing the door, taking a second to get his story straight. Once he came up with a satisfying excuse, he continued into the kitchen. There, Adam found his mother at the stove, preparing dinner for the evening.

Adam's mother turned to face him. "Miss the bus on the way home?"

"Yeah, had to have Ken bring me home," Adam said with a sigh, hoping she wouldn't ask too many questions.

"What kept you?"

Adam hoped his poker face was convincing enough to hide his annoyance. "I was wrapped up in finishing an assignment for Mr. Gardin. I didn't want to have to bring it home."

Adam's mother turned back to the stove. "As long as it doesn't become a habit."

He fought not to roll his eyes. "Can I hitch a ride into town with you when you go to work tomorrow?"

"What for?" his mother asked curiously.

"I'm meeting up with Ken, and I'd like to get some breakfast from the gas station," Adam replied readily. *See if she takes it.*

His mother thought for a moment, then shrugged. "I don't see why not. Will you need a ride home?"

"No," he said simply, trying to hide his triumphant glee. "What time should I be home?"

"Not staying over?"

"Not this time." He hoped once more that she wouldn't ask why.

"Before dark, then," his mother said simply.

Adam grinned. "Thanks, Mom!" He headed upstairs to his room.

BEFORE ADAM KNEW IT, he was at the gas station, with his mother telling him to have fun before she headed off to the post office. He hadn't been entirely untruthful about wanting breakfast from the gas station restaurant. Adam went in and got himself a breakfast sandwich and some orange juice, then sat and ate quietly. He wondered what was in store for him that day. Still, his mind often came back to everything he had seen the day before. It seemed with Cassie, anything was possible.

The gas station was in the center of town, whilst the school and the woods were on the outskirts. Adam checked a clock on the wall and guessed that by the time he reached them, it would be half past nine. With nothing better to do, he left the gas station and made his way across the streets and sidewalks of town until, at last, he came to the edge of the woods, almost exactly where Cassie entered at the end of every school day. He looked across the street to the cafeteria parking lot, finding it barren.

"You're here early," a voice said from behind him.

Adam jumped and whirled around. Cassie stood a few feet inside the woods, dressed in her usual baggy clothes.

"Did I scare you?" she asked with a playful grin.

"A little," Adam answered, embarrassed. His heart was racing. *We're alone. Completely alone. Together.*

"Sorry, I thought you'd have heard me coming," Cassie said with a contrite shrug.

"I didn't." *Say something a bit more interesting next time, dumbass.*

Cassie didn't seem bothered by his shyness. She grinned. "Follow me. I want to show you something." Without explanation, she turned around and took off jogging into the woods.

Obediently, Adam followed suit. She ran along a trail for a minute or so before veering off. He kept up with her easily, despite the odd root or low-hanging branch. Eventually, they reached a sizeable clearing around a shallow pit beneath a large fallen tree leaning at an angle.

Cassie slowed to a walk as they entered the clearing. "This is what I like to think of as my private grove. I found it not long after I moved here."

"Do you always go exploring woods by your house?" Adam asked, slightly out of breath from the jog, unlike Cassie.

She shrugged. "I always go exploring, but this is the first time I've lived near the woods." Before Adam could reply, Cassie climbed onto the fallen tree with astonishing agility, then perched herself between two limbs about ten feet above the ground.

Adam stayed where he was, unsure of what to do.

"Are you shy?" she asked.

Unable to talk around the lump in his throat, Adam nodded slowly, feeling a flush creep up his cheeks.

"It's kinda cute," Cassie said with a playful giggle.

Adam's cheeks could hardly get any redder.

Cassie lay back on the limb she was sitting on. "Why don't we play twenty questions to get to know each other?"

"Okay," Adam said awkwardly.

"I'll start. How old are you?"

"Sixteen."

"Same as me," Cassie said with a grin as she turned to look at him. "Your turn."

"Ummm…" There were hundreds of questions running through Adam's mind. *Probably better to not get too personal right away.* "Where did you move here from?"

"Valparaiso."

"So not too far."

"You kidding? It's like a different world over here," Cassie said as she spread her arms.

"How so?"

"People don't think they're inner-city gangsters, for one. For another, the school population is a lot smaller. This town is tiny compared to Valpo." Cassie grinned and added, "Don't worry. I won't count that as one of your questions."

"Oh…right. Your turn, then," Adam said, blushing again.

The game went on for an hour or so. Adam told Cassie about his family, from his truck-driver father and mail-carrier mother to his older sister who had moved out six years prior and was now married. In turn, he learned Cassie was adopted at the age of seven and lived with her real estate agent mother and lawyer father. Adam was slightly embarrassed when he realized most of his questions simply mirrored Cassie's, but she didn't seem to care.

"So, how many girlfriends have you had?" Cassie asked.

Adam leaned against a thin tree at the edge of the clearing. "Not one," he admitted.

"Really?" Cassie gasped in surprise, turning to look at him from her perch.

"Mhm," Adam confirmed. "What about boyfriends for you?"

"None."

"How…?" Adam blurted out, flabbergasted. *There is no way.*

Cassie giggled. "Don't act so surprised. You're cute and you're sweet. I'd ask you the same thing."

"Well…I've always been kind of an outsider. I mean, I've never even…well…" Adam hesitated before admitting, "I've never even kissed a girl before."

Cassie giggled again, but then her smile faltered.

"What is it?"

Cassie didn't answer right away. She seemed to be thinking, her brow furrowed. "I suppose you want to know why I've never had a boyfriend?" she said as she sat up, her cheeks suddenly pink.

"I...I'm just surprised is all. If you're embarrassed, you don't have to tell me," Adam said quickly.

Cassie looked at him, a hint of hesitation playing across her face. Then she sighed. "Any guy would be embarrassed to admit he'd never kissed a girl. It's only fair that I share something embarrassing in return." Before Adam could argue, Cassie pulled her hooded sweatshirt off and tossed it aside. Underneath, she was wearing a purple tank top, but at once, Adam understood why Cassie wore baggy clothes everywhere. She wasn't simply a pretty face. Cassie was breathtakingly gorgeous. He took in her curves at a glance but immediately sought her face. Her cheeks were a deep red, and her lustrous eyes were fixed on him, as though awaiting his reaction.

She's afraid.

"I think I get it," Adam said simply, thinking of what Damien and Ken had said about Cassie earlier that week. His heart ached for her.

"Do you?" Cassie kicked her legs. "Ever since I became a teenager, everyone has looked at me differently. It's like they don't see a person, just a sex doll."

"I'm sorry. Why don't you put the hoodie back on?" Adam suggested.

She blinked in surprise. "What?"

His cheeks burned once again. "Well, I don't want you to be uncomfortable..."

Cassie looked to be in shock. She blinked a few times but then shrugged. "Honestly, I feel better without it."

"If you're sure...," Adam mumbled, his voice trailing off. He knew all too well how most guys behaved toward girls like Cassie. Despite himself, he couldn't help but wonder if someone had taken it too far, like the jock gang had tried to. "Is that also why you learned how to fight?"

Cassie's lips twitched for a moment as she thought about her answer. "Yeah, I guess."

Adam had a dozen questions about her fighting skills alone, but he didn't have many of his twenty questions left. Silence hung between them for a moment until he finally said, "It's your turn, you know."

Cassie blinked and chuckled. "Right, I almost forgot. Hmmm..." She sat up and ran a hand through her hair as she thought. Cassie stared off for a moment and then finally looked back at him. "Why don't you come up here and sit with me?"

Adam blinked in surprise. "Well...I mean...yeah, okay." He walked over to the base of the tree and made his way up to where Cassie was sitting.

She smiled. "That's better, isn't it?"

Adam nodded, but there was a new tension in the air now that they were so close together. He sat on a branch opposite her, while she lounged between her two branches, watching him with those shining blue eyes.

"All right, my turn," Adam declared.

Cassie waved her hand as if to say, "Go ahead."

Adam thought about his question carefully. He didn't want to come off as suspicious, but he wanted to know. "Why did you decide to hang out with me?"

Cassie's smile faltered for a moment, and Adam's heart clenched. He'd said the wrong thing. However, she flipped her hair and sighed.

"I thought that would be obvious." When Adam frowned, she chuckled. "You'd just risked your neck to save me. That's a good way to get a girl's attention."

Adam blushed furiously. "Well, I couldn't just do nothing..."

Cassie's smile faded again. "In a bigger town, I'm not sure anyone would have noticed."

Adam felt another tightness in his chest. The unspoken question reared its ugly head again in the silence between them, but he didn't have the courage to ask. *If it did happen, she shouldn't have to relive it for my sake.*

"Please don't look at me like that."

Adam blinked. "Like...like what?"

"The pity. The sad eyes. Please don't."

Cassie was polite, but there was something in her words that ate at him. Still, Adam wouldn't press the matter. He looked away. "I'm sorry..."

"It's just..." Cassie shifted uncomfortably between her two branches.

"Don't worry. I understand," he said to console her.

"Do you?" Cassie raised an eyebrow.

Adam's eyes met hers. He could only imagine how other people had looked at her over the years. She was strong now, but somehow Adam knew she hadn't always been. Cassie was strong now because she had had to be, and pitying her took her back to that time before she had learned to rise above whatever had happened to her. He didn't want her to feel that pain again. The idea of it was like a weight in his chest.

"Yes, I do."

Cassie seemed taken aback by his sincerity. Her eyes widened and her brow furrowed, but she said nothing. Instead, she climbed out of her spot on the tree. Adam thought she was going to jump down and walk away, but then she sat down next to him. She leaned against him lightly, though her eyes were downcast.

"What is it?" he asked.

Cassie bit her lip before answering. "You might just be the sweetest person I've ever met."

Adam's cheeks flared up immediately. "Really?"

Cassie looked at him and nodded. "Really."

His heart ached for her. With Cassie so close, he was almost overcome by the urge to pull her into his arms and hold her, but he doubted she would appreciate it. To his surprise, she leaned more firmly into his chest and rested her forehead against his cheek.

"You don't know how special you are."

The touch of her skin against his seemed to send a wave throughout his body. Adam almost couldn't breathe or think. What was happening to him? Despite his misgivings, he slid his arms around her gently. But she didn't pull away.

Adam had no idea how long he held Cassie like that. It could have been mere minutes, or perhaps even hours. They were silent the whole time, but it was a peaceful quiet. Adam dared to hope that he had had the calming effect on her he had wanted to offer.

"You're not the only one who can read people," she whispered.

Adam looked down at her. "What do you mean?"

Cassie smiled up at him, her eyes shining brilliantly. Her face was inches from his own. "It's how I knew you meant what you said. I think we have a lot in common."

Adam grinned nervously. "Oh yeah?"

Cassie touched a hand to his cheek. "Yes, I do."

Adam was amazed at how anyone's skin could be so soft. Her touch was gentle, but it sent a strange sensation throughout his body that was unlike anything he had ever experienced. It was a warm feeling tinged with a hint of excitement. Adam leaned his head into her palm, closing his eyes for a moment to savor the sweet sensation it gave him.

Then Cassie whispered silkily, "Can I kiss you, Adam?"

"Wh-what?"

Cassie didn't say anything, merely looking at him with her questioning eyes as she bit her lip. For a moment, Adam hesitated, fearing things were moving too fast, but the way she looked at him and the closeness between them were too much to resist. Before he could rethink his decision, he threw caution to the winds and kissed her.

The world fell away immediately. Adam forgot about the tree bark pressing into his back, the wind gently ruffling his short hair, or even the overcast light all around them. In that moment, all he felt were Cassie's lips. They were as soft as the hand on his cheek, and her breath was sweet. Her lips parted slightly, and his own reacted in a way that felt so natural, he might have been practicing for the moment his entire life. *This...This is heaven.*

Slowly, they pulled apart. Adam looked into her eyes as Ken's warning echoed in his head. *Don't get too attached too quickly.* His own thoughts argued, *But she's so amazing! She's smart, she's perceptive, and she's possibly the most beautiful girl alive!*

Cassie's voice interrupted his internal argument. "How was that?" she asked sweetly.

Adam took a deep breath. "A-amazing."

Cassie giggled. "I'm glad." She rested her head back against his cheek.

Once again, Adam lost track of time. He was lost between the feeling of Cassie against him and reliving their first kiss over and over in his mind. Whatever questions had remained were completely forgotten. If they never left that spot, Adam wasn't sure he would mind.

Then his phone buzzed. Heaving a sigh, he reached into his pocket and pulled it out, finding a text from Ken. *I'm in the cafeteria parking lot.*

"Your ride?" Cassie asked, looking up at him.

Adam couldn't hide his disappointment at their time being at an end. With another sigh, he replied, "Yeah. I gotta be heading home." He got up and climbed down from the tree.

Cassie jumped down after him. "Do you want to do this again next week?"

Adam froze momentarily, his heart leaping. "Sure!" His cheeks burned—his reply had been far too eager.

Cassie giggled. "Are we just gonna sit in the tree and cuddle all day again?"

Adam chuckled, although the idea didn't sound half bad to him. "Or maybe you can teach me how to fight."

Cassie smiled. "I could, actually."

Adam's face burned once again. "That was a joke…"

"But I could! Haven't you ever wanted to learn?"

Adam shrugged. "I mean, my friends are all into it. They fight for fun."

"But you don't?"

"Well, I'm not very good…"

Cassie shoved his shoulder playfully. "Neither was I. Come on, by the time I'm through with you, you'll be able to beat them all at once!"

Adam chuckled. "All right, you're on. See you Monday, then?"

"Hold on."

Adam turned to look at her once again. Cassie stepped up to him.

"Aren't you gonna kiss me goodbye?"

Any excuse to kiss you again works for me! Embarrassed at his own thought, Adam opened his mouth to speak, but then Cassie was pressing her lips to his. Just as before, Adam completely lost himself to her. Ken, his ride home, and everything else faded away as he floated back into the paradise her kiss pulled him into.

Then, unfortunately, it was over.

Cassie pulled away and whispered sweetly, "See you Monday."

Adam smiled and turned away, heading back toward the school. Ken would undoubtedly have a ton of questions, but he'd deal with that when the time came. For now, Adam savored every second they had spent in the woods together. *She really is amazing.*

6. The Will of the Shadow

After watching Adam leave in silence, Cassie climbed back up to her spot in the tree between the two large branches and stretched out, staring up at the dusk sky. She loved it there. The trees around the grove were thick enough to hide it from sight for twenty feet or so, while still allowing an unobscured view of the stars. Plus, it was better than being in the house with her adoptive parents.

Cassie lay staring up at the darkening sky, her lips curling into a confident half smile as she recounted the day's events. Everything was going perfectly. There were a few moments when Asmodeous had spoken to her, but Adam didn't seem to notice her distraction. Plus, the advice Asmodeous had given had paid dividends. *Establish trust,* he had said. *Every embarrassing fact he puts forth, give him one of your own.* However, the cuddling and kissing had been all her idea. Once she had figured out Adam wouldn't try to force himself on her, seducing him seemed almost too easy.

Still, Cassie couldn't deny that she appreciated how he looked at her. He might have been the first person in Corbanton to see her without her pullover on, but his eyes didn't linger. Sure, he had looked at first, but who wouldn't? Hell, Cassie herself would have looked.

But when his eyes had met hers the moment after, there was no hunger or lust, just understanding with a hint of pity. Cassie sighed. She had dealt with those sad stares through most of her time at the orphanage, especially when she would meet potential adopters. They always heard her story and always looked at her with those dismal, pathetic eyes.

Cassie's breath caught and her heart accelerated. She sat bolt upright and looked around the grove, her eyes wide. Goosebumps broke out on her skin, and she quietly reminded herself that she was here in her grove, not back where *it* had happened. The pitying eyes of those around her always threatened to take her back to the worst night of her life, a night she'd spent thirteen years trying to forget.

Think about what you did today. Think about what's going on right now. You're doing great. You're finally repaying your debt to him.

Cassie stretched back out on the branch, wrangling her thoughts under control. Yes, things were going her way at last. In a hundred years, she could never repay her debt for all Asmodeous had done for her since *that* night. Going through with his plan seemed like such a little thing by comparison, but it was all he had asked of her. It was a small price, and she was more than willing to pay it.

You underestimate the importance of what you are doing.

Cassie sighed. Asmodeous didn't often interrupt her thoughts. Sometimes, she even forgot he knew what she was thinking. He didn't speak to her often, but she always knew he was there. That was enough for her. *Compared to what you've done for me, it seems like nothing,* she thought in reply.

Your perspective is too limited. In time, you will understand.

Cassie didn't argue. Patience was probably Asmodeous's most extolled virtue. *"Anything could be achieved if given enough time,"* he would say. All things came with time, but for Cassie, the waiting was the hardest part.

With a frustrated sigh as darkness fell over the woods, Cassie slipped back into her pullover and jumped down from her perch to head home. She hated waiting: waiting for a family to take her home, waiting for Kaleb to be punished, waiting for Adam to open up to her fully…

Cassie trudged through the woods, her thoughts trailing off. *Adam*—he really was a sweet boy. He seemed genuinely concerned about how uncomfortable she was, and his embrace had been warm and consoling. Even the kissing had been strangely electrifying. Despite her earlier trepidation over courting him, she was looking forward to her next opportunity to pull him a little closer. *Got to admit that it's kind of fun.*

Cassie reached the edge of the woods, and her eyes burned with hate. Kaleb's car was parked in the driveway. As she approached the front door, she asked Asmodeous for what felt like the thousandth time: *Promise that he'll get what's coming to him?*

As usual, Asmodeous's cold and simple answer made her heart leap with resentful glee. *He will.*

Cassie stepped inside, finding Darcy waiting for her. Her arms were folded, her expression severe. "And where have you been, young lady?"

Cassie blinked. This was unusual for Darcy. "Umm...in the woods across the street?"

"Alone, until this hour?"

Cassie frowned. "It's barely eight o'clock. This isn't Valpo. Nothing happens here."

The moment the words left her mouth, Cassie regretted it.

Darcy fired back, "I'm sure that's what your sister thought the night your dad..." Then her eyes widened, and she covered her mouth in horror.

Cassie's hands clenched into fists. It was as though she was falling down a dark tunnel, surrounded by screams and cries of hate and malice. She could almost hear *him* calling her name, blood dripping from a kitchen knife held over the body of...

Darcy's arms wrapping around her snapped Cassie out of her flashback. "Honey, I'm sorry! I'm so, so sorry! I just...I worry! Moving back here, it...it wasn't a good idea. We should go somewhere else far from here."

Cassie stiffened. What little of the fog had been left from the flashback disappeared entirely at Darcy's suggestion. *No, I'm too close. Adam's in our grasp. I can't let him slip away.* "Mom," Cassie said quietly, "it's okay. I'm fine."

"No, no, you're not," Darcy insisted tearfully. "None of us are. Your father and I have both worried about you since coming back here..."

It took all of Cassie's will not to shiver with revulsion when Darcy referred to Kaleb as her father. *Speak of the devil...*

Kaleb stepped into view from the hallway, his brow wrinkled with concern. "What's this all about?"

Cassie glared at him with all of the venom she could muster, then answered as calmly as she could manage, "Nothing, it's fine."

Kaleb recoiled and looked away.

Darcy let go and stammered, "I...I got worried when Cassie came home so late. I...I brought up *that* night..."

Kaleb looked at her in shock. "Darcy! You know we can't do that to her!"

As if you actually care, Cassie thought spitefully.

"I know, I know!" Darcy sobbed before turning and heading down the hall to their bedroom. "I...I need a moment."

Cassie might have felt bad for Darcy, maybe even had a little affection for her...if she wasn't so stupidly blind to the monster Kaleb was.

Once the bedroom door closed, Kaleb opened his mouth to speak, but Cassie cut him off. "Don't. Say. A word."

Kaleb narrowed his eyes in frustration. "She's just trying to protect you."

Cassie folded her arms. If she wasn't so angry, she might have laughed. "Yet she has no idea what she really needs to be protecting me from." She wished her eyes could drill holes straight into Kaleb's skull, putting him out of her life forever.

A vein pulsed in Kaleb's temple. Through gritted teeth, he whispered, "Just let it go, Cassie!"

Every muscle in Cassie's body screamed to lash out at him, but Asmodeous's words whispered softly through her mind. *Not yet.*

Cassie stepped around him and hissed, "Maybe when you stop getting off on the idea of fucking your so-called 'daughter,' I will." Though she wouldn't look at him, Cassie imagined with cruel satisfaction the shocked look on his face as she went down the hall and into her room, locking the door behind her.

She sat down on her bed, unable to stop herself from smiling triumphantly. As if things going so well with Adam wasn't enough, throwing Kaleb's depravity in his face had made that day the best for Cassie in a long time. Maybe if she stuck it to him hard enough, he might feel a fraction of the pain he heaped on her those three years ago, when his intentions became clear.

You should not provoke him like that.

Why not? Cassie frowned, looking at her shadow on the floor beside her bed. *He can't touch me. If I don't take him down, he'll still have to deal with you.*

Do not forget that I won't be with you for much longer.

Cassie's smile faltered. Truth be told, she *had* forgotten. Asmodeous was right. He was always right. As satisfying as pushing Kaleb's buttons was, it would probably be best if she didn't do it too often or too hard...at least until he was dealt with properly.

Instead, focus on the task at hand.

Right. Cassie took a deep breath and went over her time with Adam in her head once more. Within seconds, her smile had returned. She was proud of how she had taken control after just a few tips from Asmodeous, finally getting Adam to open up to her. The rest was coming to her pretty easily.

Cassie pulled off her hooded sweatshirt and tossed it aside before standing in front of her mirror. She looked herself up and down, then placed a hand on her hip and struck a pose like she'd seen on countless magazine covers. A surge of confidence ran through her. Adam wouldn't be able to resist her. *Of course, he'd go for a girl like me. Hell,* I'd *go for a girl like me.*

At that thought, Cassie's mind wandered over some of the girls she'd seen since coming to Corbanton High School. She'd been so focused on finding a boy to suit Asmodeous's needs, she hadn't paid too much attention to the girls, but there were more than a few cute ones she wouldn't mind getting to know a little better. Still, one step at a time. *Adam's pretty cute too. Guess we could have done much worse.*

Cassie sat back down on the bed, blushing a little but still smiling. This was going to be way more fun than she had first thought.

"CASSIE, COME OUT, WHEREVER you are!" Sam was calling.

Cassie sat under a desk, hugging her knees to her chest. Daddy's voice didn't sound like that. Daddy was funny and kind, but Daddy was gone. It was Sam now.

She watched as Sam used a butcher's knife to saw Mommy's head off. Then he saw her.

Cassie ran. She'd run like she'd never run before. Sam chased her. He made the whole family chase her, even though they were already dead. Then Ally came home. Ally found her, but Sam found them too. He never put down the knife. It was still covered in Mommy's blood. Carol and Chad were both dead. Sam had said so. Then, Sam got Ally, and as Cassie climbed out of the secret tunnel in the cellar, she saw Ally lying face down in a pool of blood, her eyes wide and empty.

Cassie hadn't screamed the whole night until that moment. Then she screamed. She screamed louder and harder than she had ever screamed before. They were all dead. Everyone she'd ever known.

Cassie woke up tangled in her bed sheets and bathed in sweat. Her heart raced in her chest, and she was lightheaded from breathing so rapidly. She reached across to her nightstand and clicked on a little lamp. Its light chased away the shadows holding the ghosts of *that* night—the night her family died. It had been some time since she'd had a nightmare about it, but Darcy bringing it up tonight must've stirred the memories. Cassie sat up in bed and hugged her knees, trembling violently.

She spotted the hooded shadow against the wall. Asmodeous didn't often take his own shape around her, but she guessed it was no big deal with them being alone. His presence was comforting. He had saved her that night. Asmodeous had destroyed Sam, and Cassie had let him into her shadow like he'd asked. He'd watched out for her ever since, scaring away bullies at the orphanage, warning her of guys who would try to take advantage of her like Kaleb did, and teaching her how to look out for herself. Asmodeous had always been there for her.

He spoke aloud, slightly above a whisper, "Now that we have come this far, perhaps it is time for you to know what will happen next."

Cassie looked at where she imagined his eyes to be. "What do you mean? Did you wake me up for this?"

"No, you awoke of your own accord."

Cassie wasn't sure if she believed that. She had never had an easy time coming out of flashback nightmares on her own, not even when she realized she was dreaming.

However, Asmodeous continued, "I saw your dream and your thoughts that came with it."

Cassie tried not to think about it, but for a moment, she could see Ally's wide, staring, and lifeless eyes. She blinked tears away and whispered back, "What does that have to do with what happens next?"

Silence hung between them for a moment. Cassie's hair prickled. He was choosing his words carefully. Her stomach churned. Whatever he was about to say, she wasn't going to like it.

"Once this stage is complete, we must return to Corbant Manor."

Cassie's blood turned to ice. The name of her childhood home echoed in her mind, spoken not just by Asmodeous's voice, but also the people at the adoption agency, the Corbanton police, and Sam. "No...," she whimpered, her nails digging into her shins. "No, please!" Cassie choked as her breathing accelerated beyond what even the dream had caused. She buried her face in her knees and rocked back and forth, her eyes wide as she pleaded, "Please don't make me go back there!"

Asmodeous's voice whispered from right beside her. "It must be done. There is much there that cannot be substituted."

Cassie shook her head. "No. I'll go somewhere else, anywhere else. Just not there. Please don't make me go back there! Please? Please!" Tears spilled from her eyes, and Cassie hugged her knees tighter.

"There is no other way. Trust in me, and all things will be set right."

Cassie couldn't answer. The pain in her chest swallowed her words, and all she could do was cry in agony and despair. That night had left wounds in her heart and mind that never healed. Asmodeous said no more, letting Cassie cry in silence.

When at last her tears were spent, Cassie looked up at where Asmodeous's shadow had been, but there was nothing. He had returned to her own shadow, as he always did once he had said all he needed to. Cassie stared at the now-empty wall, trying to collect her thoughts through the hellish memories Asmodeous's revelation had stirred up.

Sure, she had had happy memories in her childhood home, but the ghost named Sam had shattered all of that when he had driven her father to suicide and possessed his corpse to slaughter the entire family. Cassie had thought Sam was her friend, but Asmodeous had told her the truth: Sam had been the son of the man who had built the mansion, and his spirit was responsible for driving almost all of the Corbant family to death and misery. Because of him, the mansion teemed with the trapped spirits of Cassie's family and anyone else unfortunate enough to die within its walls. His cruelty was only stopped when Cassie had let Asmodeous out of his prison beneath the mansion.

Cassie recalled how Asmodeous had ripped Sam out of her father's body and destroyed him. She was certain that if Asmodeous hadn't intervened, Sam would have killed her too. Cassie thought about all the times throughout her life Asmodeous had protected her from the likes of Kaleb, the jocks, or worse. She was always able to count on him intervening before something horrible happened. He was always there.

Trust in me, he had said.

Cassie looked down at her arms wrapped around her knees. Asmodeous had done so much for her ever since that terrible night. She owed him everything, from her life to her innocence, and much more besides. He'd asked so little of her since that night as well.

She held up a hand and counted his requests on her fingers. First, he had asked to live in her shadow. Then, he had asked her to make Kaleb move them all to Corbanton. Finally, he had asked her to find a boy like Adam. This request was only the fourth he had made of her.

Cassie took a deep breath and crossed her legs, her trembling easing. It seemed like such a small thing in light of all he had done for her. Sure, it was agonizing, but compared to what he had saved her from, surely it could be so much worse. She shuddered at the thought. But he was asking much less than what she owed to him. It wouldn't be fair to refuse.

Cassie turned to face the opposite wall. It wasn't difficult to imagine Corbant Manor off in the direction she was facing, looming out of the darkness of the trees surrounding it, like a grim obelisk, a monument to all the pain and suffering that had occurred within its walls. Still, if Asmodeous asked her to go back to where it all began, she could not bring herself to say no.

7. The Unlikely Paramour

Adam and company were gathered on the couches in the entrance hallway of the school, as usual, passing the time before classes began. So far, Ken was the only one who knew about what had happened with Cassie in the woods. Adam had withheld the information from the rest of his friend group because he wasn't entirely sure what they'd think of it just yet.

They chatted and bantered as normal until Cassie walked around the corner and came toward them, calling cheerfully, "Hey, Adam!"

The conversation stopped immediately. All five pairs of eyes went wide and turned in Cassie's direction. Though she was still concealed beneath her baggy clothes, her demeanor had shifted more toward how she had behaved when they were alone in the woods. She walked up to Adam and took his hand.

"Aren't you going to sit with me before class?"

"I...Why...Why would I do that?" he stammered, dumbfounded.

She giggled and pulled him up off the couch. "Isn't that what you do with your girlfriend?"

What did she just say? Adam's legs suddenly didn't want to work anymore.

Cassie had said it loud enough to get the attention of everyone in the hallway. There were at least a dozen other students there, and they all fell silent, gawking in disbelief.

"I...I guess," he said meekly, letting himself be dragged to their first class.

People stared as they passed—Cassie grinning broadly, while Adam blushed and hurried along behind her, their hands clasped.

At last, they entered Mr. Martinez's classroom. Cassie led him to the seat next to hers and pulled the chair out for him.

Despite his shock, Adam was forced to admit Cassie's excited antics were rather adorable. He sat next to her, and she scooted her chair closer to his.

"So...am I really your boyfriend now?" he asked.

Cassie giggled, leaned back in her chair, and covered her mouth before whispering conspiratorially, "Of course, silly. I wouldn't kiss just anybody."

"I...I just...I thought..."

"You thought what?" Cassie tilted her head and fluttered her eyelashes.

"I...I dunno what I thought," Adam mumbled, no idea what else to say.

Cassie's smile faltered a little. "You are okay with me saying we're boyfriend and girlfriend, right?"

Adam was speechless. The suddenness of it all coupled with the titles ringing in his ears left his head spinning. *Girlfriend. She's my girlfriend. She wants to be my girlfriend.* He smiled at her. "Well, yeah! Of course, I am! It just...caught me off guard is all."

Cassie giggled and flipped her hair. "Feel like Saturday was some kind of fever dream or something?"

Adam blinked. *On the nose with that one.* "Well...I mean...yeah."

She pushed his shoulder playfully. "Don't worry about it. I really do like you."

"I...I like you too," he said quietly. This was too good to be true. How could she possibly want to be his girlfriend? They had as many common interests as some of his closest friends, and he couldn't deny how beautiful she was. Cassie could easily do better than him. Was any of this real?

Then Cassie whispered, "By the way, I will teach you how to fight. This Saturday, same time, same place. All right?"

"I'll be there."

Shortly after their exchange, other students began walking in. Every one of them paused and looked confused when they saw Adam and Cassie side by side. Cassie gave his hand a squeeze and let her eyes wander, seemingly oblivious to the stares. Adam squeezed back, letting his eyes do the same, despite his red face. Apparently, everyone thought he was as unlikely to be with Cassie as he was. Mr. Martinez came in soon after, paying no mind to the altered seating arrangement, and went about class as usual.

Afterward, Adam and Cassie walked together to the next, though they didn't share it. Cassie left Adam at the door and called, "See you again soon!" Then she flipped her hair and smiled at him before heading off to her own class.

Adam could barely breathe. *This has to be a dream.* It was impossible for him to wrap his mind around the idea that Cassie was into him. She was gorgeous, and he was...mediocre at best. Cassie dominated his thoughts all the way through class—until the bell rang and he headed out the door to find her standing there, waiting for him and smiling brightly.

The morning passed in a haze for Adam. The only thing he could clearly think about was Cassie. She walked with him from each class to the next, completely unbothered by the stares and whispers of other students. Adam, on the other hand, was far from accustomed to the attention. He had spent years making himself scarce, going from class to class as quickly as possible without drawing attention to himself, but now Cassie's presence seemed to have turned a spotlight onto his every move. His only escape was to focus solely on Cassie, but that had dangers of its own. Every time she left him in a classroom, he felt a pang of longing to be back with her.

Finally, the bell rang for lunch. This time, Cassie did not meet Adam at the door. Slightly puzzled but unperturbed, he went to his locker to get his lunch and made for the cafeteria. His usual table was empty, so he took his seat as normal and waited for the rest of his gang to arrive.

"What. The. Hell," Damien's voice came from behind him as he set his lunch tray down on Adam's left side.

"What?" Adam asked, though he already knew the answer.

"Did she really just grab you off the couch and declare you her boyfriend?" Damien asked, aghast as he fell into his seat.

Adam shrugged. "I mean, we hung out over the weekend, so it's not completely out of the blue."

Damien looked offended. "How come I didn't hear about this?"

Adam shrugged again. "I didn't think anything would come of it."

Walter arrived next, seating himself opposite Adam. Without hesitation, he asked, "How the hell did you pull that one off?"

"I'm not sure," Adam admitted truthfully.

"You know you are the envy of every guy in school right now," Ken added, sitting down beside Walter, opposite Damien.

"I...I hadn't thought of that," Adam stammered, blushing yet again.

"Literally. Some guys would kill to be you right now." Walter eyed him with a bizarre reverence Adam found both comedic and off-putting.

"Congratulations, man," Lex said with a smile, sitting down on Walter's opposite side.

"Thanks," Adam mumbled.

The conversation stopped abruptly as Lex, Walter, and Ken all turned to look in the same direction behind Adam. He turned in his seat. Cassie was coming toward them, tray in hand. She sat down in the empty chair on Adam's right.

"Hey guys! Sorry for stealing Adam so abruptly this morning." She seemed perfectly at ease, even though both Walter and Damien's mouths were agape.

"He seemed like he was enjoying himself," Ken said with a sly smile at Adam.

"Were you?" Cassie turned to face Adam with a flip of her hair.

"I...I was just taken by surprise is all." Adam's blush returned with a vengeance.

"I didn't mean to embarrass you," Cassie said apologetically. "I just got a little over-excited. You are my first boyfriend, after all."

"Are you serious?" Walter blurted out.

"Yes, I am," Cassie said with another light flip of her hair. "You'd be surprised how hard it is to find a guy that doesn't treat me like a walking sex toy."

Ken snorted slightly in laughter. Adam didn't look, but he knew Damien was glaring at Ken.

"So how did you two meet anyway?" Walter asked eagerly.

Adam opened his mouth for a moment but then closed it again. He tried but couldn't find the words to explain how it had all happened.

Cassie said casually, "Oh, he just chased me in the woods."

Ken snorted again, and Adam was mortified.

Walter's eyes bulged from his head, and he dropped his fork. "Are you serious?"

Cassie laughed. "He was warning me about a gang of jocks coming after me."

Damien finally took his eyes off Cassie to look at Adam in shock. "So, it was you who beat the shit out of those guys!"

"Actually—"

Cassie interrupted him. "We did it together."

Lex, Damien, and Walter gasped collectively. Ken looked at Adam, his eyes narrowed.

Adam appeared just as shocked as the other three. He turned to Cassie to protest, but she smiled at him and winked before continuing.

"Yeah, there was no way I could have taken all five of them down if two hadn't had to hold him down."

"So...while two held Adam down, you knocked the other three around?" Walter questioned, aghast.

Adam finally found his voice. "I don't think they were expecting her to put up a fight at all."

Lex nodded in understanding. "Of course not."

"So, after the first one went down, I had already finished the second before the third did anything. Nice and smooth." Cassie popped a grape into her mouth.

"Are you a blackbelt or something?" Walter asked.

"Nah, I just like to fight."

Walter was in awe, and Lex nodded, clearly impressed.

Damien mused aloud, "I'm surprised the guys' parents haven't raised hell about it."

"I guarantee their parents never got the full story," Adam said. The thought hadn't occurred to him until that moment, but he doubted it was anything but the truth.

"Yeah, they'd never admit to chasing a girl into the woods, only to get the shit beat out of them by said girl," Ken observed.

The bell rang, and Adam and Cassie headed off to their next class together. Much to Adam's disappointment, this class had assigned seating, as did the third class he and Cassie had together. Even so, he still found it difficult to take his eyes off of her. Every glance he snuck in her direction seemed to indicate she felt the same about him. Their eyes met on several occasions, and she'd smile subtly. Then Adam would look away and try in vain to focus on class.

When at last the day's end bell rang, they walked to each other's lockers and then headed for the cafeteria doors.

"Which bus is yours?" Cassie asked, scanning the parking lot.

"It's at the very back of the lot on the far right," Adam answered, pointing the way.

"I'll walk there with you. It's not out of my way," Cassie said cheerfully with another of her hair flips, which Adam was quickly becoming fond of. She followed him to his bus while other students stared out the windows of the other buses in the lot.

Adam assumed they were just as surprised to see them together as he was. When he reached the bus, he turned to her and said, "So...see you tomorrow?"

"Of course," Cassie replied with a grin, then kissed him.

Adam hadn't been ready. His breath seemed to vanish immediately, as did the rest of the world around them. It was over in an instant, but to Adam, it could have lasted an eternity.

Cassie smiled at him and headed across the street toward the woods. Adam shook his head to clear the fog her kiss had left over and climbed the bus steps, still not believing the day had happened.

The week went by, and the entire school was abuzz. Adam Sullivan, the awkward shy nerd, was dating Cassie Ebonwood, the mysterious but undeniably attractive new girl. Looks and whispers followed them wherever they went. Adam wasn't sure he would ever get used to it. If he hadn't been so entranced by Cassie's presence, he might have found the will to hate the stares. They passed each day much as they had Monday, with Cassie joining Adam and his friends both before their first class and during lunch. She fit in easily, much to Adam's delight.

When Saturday arrived, with similar arrangements to the previous week, Adam was once again alone in the woods. He found his way to Cassie's grove easily. Though he was early, Cassie didn't leave him waiting for long. She showed up just as she did the previous weekend, baggy clothes and all.

Cassie stepped up to him and smiled. "So, ready to learn how to fight?"

Adam chuckled. "Getting right down to business, eh?"

Cassie giggled. "Or was there something else on your mind?"

Adam blushed a little. "Well, not really."

Cassie placed a hand on his cheek and kissed the opposite. "That's what I like about you."

Adam's cheeks burned. "What, that I can't think clearly when you're around?"

Cassie stepped back with a chuckle. "No, silly. That you don't have an ulterior motive or hidden agenda." She pulled her hoodie off, revealing nothing but a black sports bra. Cassie kicked off her shoes and stepped out of her pants, showing a pair of black athletic leggings underneath. The fabric clung to her long, muscular legs, accentuating every detail of her form. For the first time since meeting her, Adam lost himself in the perfection of her shape.

When he realized he had been staring, Adam looked away, mentally chastising himself. Cassie's hand returned to his cheek, turning his face back toward hers. She looked at him with those brilliant, crystal-blue eyes.

"Adam...it's okay."

He bit his lip. "I...I didn't want to stare." Maybe he was no better than the jocks after all? As soon as he saw the full extent of her curves, he had stared, just like everyone else. Maybe he *was* just another pervert.

Cassie sighed, tilting her head and fluttering her eyelashes. "It's okay, really."

Adam bit his lip, his breathing accelerating. Was she doing this on purpose? The tilt of her head, her outfit, the fluttering eyelashes, all lured him in. "I...I don't know."

"Listen," Cassie whispered softly, "I chose this outfit today for two reasons. First, it's kind of warm, and we're going to be moving a lot. Second...I'm ready for you to see a little more of me."

Adam shuddered slightly. Why was her whisper so tantalizing?

She continued, "You've earned my trust already. I don't feel like I have to hide with you."

Adam heaved a sigh and wrangled his thoughts back under control. "All right. I just...I don't want you to feel uncomfortable."

Cassie giggled and kissed him gently, sending waves of electricity throughout Adam's body. She whispered, "On the contrary. I like when you look at me."

Adam's heart was hammering. Her words echoed in his mind, igniting a sense of desire he was unfamiliar with. *She likes when I look at her. She* likes *it.* He smiled nervously, trying to hide the excitement surging through him.

"Let's get started, shall we?" she said with a sultry wink and a smile that drove Adam's heart into overdrive.

Within minutes, however, Adam's desires were almost completely forgotten. First, Cassie had them both stretching, and then she guided him through some basic stances and movements.

"You're kind of small like me, so agility is your friend. Flow from one move to the next," she said as they worked through one of her movement exercises.

"This is nothing like how the guys were taught," Adam observed, keeping his eyes forward, trying to banish the awkward feeling in his muscles from moving in ways they weren't accustomed.

"How were they taught?" Cassie asked, standing beside him, watching his posture and form.

"Mostly by practicing on each other."

Cassie crossed her arms, frowning. "Typical. Also, not a good way for someone without confidence to learn."

Adam blushed once more. "I know..."

Cassie walked around him as he continued his exercise. "Lack of confidence breeds hesitation, and hesitation can get you ki...er, hurt."

Adam bristled, freezing mid-movement. "You were about to say 'killed,' weren't you?"

Cassie sighed. "Yeah. That's how I was taught. Life or death."

Adam glanced at her. "Your trainer was that rough?"

Cassie chuckled. "No, that's just the mentality he pushed. No half measures, no hesitation."

"How often did you practice on him?"

"Never."

Adam was speechless. Maybe Cassie was right, and he had just been trying to learn all the wrong ways. Every time he tried with one of the guys, though, they would destroy him. He never stood a chance, and it hadn't taken long for him to start thinking he never would. Adam resumed the movement exercise, determined to keep his focus.

The lesson wore on, with Cassie teaching Adam a few simple strike combos and how to flow from one to the next. Once or twice, he got a little overzealous and lost his balance, but Cassie was patient with him.

"Take your time and learn the feel of the moves first before trying to string them all together. Practice the moves slowly until they feel as natural as breathing, and *then* work on your speed." Adam followed her instructions to the letter until, at last, Cassie said, "There, I think that's enough for today."

"How am I doing?"

"I'll be honest, you're going kinda slow, but that's probably because you've never focused on just moving before. You don't dance, do you?"

"Never have."

"That's what it is. It's a dance, only people might be trying to kill you instead of just moving to music."

"I'll try to remember that," Adam said, embarrassed.

"Don't worry. It takes time to learn. Why don't we go again tomorrow?"

"Oh...I want to," he explained, unable to hide his disappointment, "but I'm meeting with the guys to plan our annual Halloween party."

Cassie's eyes lit up. "That sounds fun!"

Adam nodded. "It's the highlight of my year. You..." He hesitated but decided to ask anyways since he had already come this far with her. "You wouldn't want to come, would you?"

"Is that an invitation?" Cassie asked, leaning forward with her hands on her hips.

Adam chuckled nervously and nodded. "Yes, it is."

Cassie walked up to him and threw her arms around his neck. "Then I accept." She then kissed him.

The moment her lips touched his, all of the desire he had almost completely forgotten from earlier that day came surging back. Their lips moved together in a way that fanned the flames within him, and every nerve was alight at the feeling of her body pressed against his.

Then, after only a few short, blissful seconds, she pulled away. Her eyes were smoldering, and for a moment, Adam considered she might be feeling the same as him. *I can't believe this is really happening. I really am the luckiest guy on earth.*

8. A Complication

Two weeks later, Cassie and Adam were cuddled together in her grove on a blanket in the shallow pit beneath the fallen tree. Adam was learning her self-defense style well, and Cassie was enjoying teaching him. To her surprise, she was growing quite comfortable around him. She could let her guard down with Adam, and she liked who she was when she felt that level of ease. It was as though he had stirred something to life in her she thought had died from all the tragedy she had endured, something that was confident and loved just to have fun and enjoy life.

Cassie lay with her head on his chest, her hand idly tracing invisible patterns on his shirt. His arm wrapped around her back, with his hand on her waist in a comfortable embrace. Her usual hoodie and oversized jeans lay at arm's length away on the ground, and Cassie was dressed in a white spaghetti-strap tank top and black yoga pants.

She looked up at him. His other arm was tucked behind his head, and his eyes were closed. The barest hint of a smile teased the corners of his lips. *I wonder what he's thinking about.*

As Cassie watched Adam, she thought about how he had treated her for the past three weeks. There was no end to his consideration for her, and if she gave any hint of being uncomfortable, he reacted without hesitation to rectify the situation. Adam might very well have been the sweetest boy alive, and despite herself, Cassie often longed to look into his dark brown eyes. There was a warmth there she wasn't familiar with, but it made her feel safe and at peace.

Adam's eyes opened, and he looked back at her with a contented half-smile. "What?"

Cassie's cheeks warmed slightly, and her heart fluttered. "Oh, just looking at you. Is that a crime?"

Adam chuckled and turned his gaze back to the sky, heaving a sigh. "Not at all."

Unable to stop a delighted giggle, Cassie resumed tracing patterns on his chest, remaining at peace in his embrace.

Remember your purpose here.

Cassie stiffened as Asmodeous's voice drifted through her head, sharp and commanding. She sat up abruptly when a chill ran down her spine.

Adam looked at her, his eyes full of concern. "What's wrong?"

Cassie glanced at him, longing to go back to mere seconds ago. Then she realized what Asmodeous was warning her away from, but it was already too late. *Shit.*

Her heart contracting, Cassie shook her head. "It...It's nothing." She got to her feet and grabbed her baggy clothes.

"Are you leaving?" Adam asked, a hint of disappointment in his voice.

Cassie bit her lip. She was halfway through slipping back into her too-large jeans. "I...I..."

"Is everything okay?" Adam sat up and turned to face her, his expression full of worry.

Cassie's heart melted...and that was the problem. She finished redressing but stopped, unwilling to cause Adam undue pain. Even with her back to him, she could feel his eyes on her. Those deep, warm, brown eyes she lost herself in every time he smiled at her.

Tears played at the corners of her own eyes, self-loathing filling her. *I'm using him, and he deserves so much better.* Pain welled in her chest as she thought of how things had started between them and what her intentions had been, but that had been before she'd gotten to know him. How could she have known the candidate Asmodeous was after would also happen to be the sweetest boy she had ever met? How could she have known that, over the course of pretending to have feelings for him, those emotions would suddenly become very, very real?

Cassie bit her lip, words unspoken filling her mouth with a bitter taste. "I...I have to tell you s-something...something that I've...never...told anyone..." *Where to begin?* Cassie thought about Asmodeous and everything that had happened to lead to this moment, including their plan for Adam. In that instant, she considered sharing her deepest secret with someone she genuinely cared about.

But Cassie couldn't do it. Despite her feelings for Adam, she couldn't bring herself to betray Asmodeous like that. He had done far too much for her, and she couldn't live with the idea of turning her back on him. Still, Adam waited in silence for whatever she was about to say. *I have to tell him* something.

She wiped her eyes with her sleeve quickly and turned to face him. Unable to dispel her air of vulnerability, Cassie decided to at least give him some truth about herself. "You...You're not like any guy I've ever met, and before you...I...I felt like...well...I was wondering about...being with a girl..."

Adam frowned. "Are you saying...you're bi?"

Cassie blushed but nodded. Even if it was nothing compared to the other secrets she was keeping from him, it was still a confession enough to ease the tension between them. Plus, at least it was true. "I...Before you, I was honestly more interested in girls. There were a few guys I didn't mind looking at but...I could never get past not wanting to be treated like a sex doll. Girls...well...There are plenty of cute ones, and they haven't really looked at me like that before, and I was kind of excited to start exploring that a bit more, but then I met you. You're just so sweet and so caring, and I...well..." Cassie's voice trailed off. She choked on words she wanted to say but couldn't.

Adam walked up to her and placed a hand on her cheek. Despite herself, her eyes filled with tears again, and she leaned into his hand. His skin wasn't the smoothest, but his touch was the most comforting sensation she had ever known. He was always gentle with her.

"It's okay, I understand."

"Do you?" she asked, looking at him once more.

"Yeah, I guess I do." Adam lowered his hand and looked at the ground. "I guess...I guess I kind of owe you a similar confession."

Cassie furrowed her brow. "What do you mean?"

Adam's cheeks flushed. "Well...one of the reasons I've always been something of a social outcast is...well, I've never really done what most guys my age do. I'm not...well...I'm not always trying to get laid or anything like that." The red in his cheeks deepened. "Truth is...I guess I just...never felt the same desire they did. To this day, I don't really understand why they obsess over it so much. Like...I guess I thought there was just something wrong with me because I always wanted...more than that...if that makes any sense."

Cassie's heart ached for him. "I've heard of people being like that before."

Adam sighed. "Around here, it's considered pretty damn weird."

"Any weirder than being into both guys and girls?" She shoved his shoulder playfully.

Adam chuckled. "I guess so. Rumors flew about me being gay for the longest time because of it."

"There are much worse things you could be than gay," Cassie pointed out.

"Yeah, but it still sucks when people make assumptions about you," Adam replied with a dejected sigh.

"Yeah, that is true..." Cassie understood that feeling all too well. Still, she didn't like seeing Adam look so crestfallen. For a moment, her own conundrum was forgotten as she stepped up to him. "I've seen the way you look at me. I'm pretty sure you're not gay."

Adam avoided her gaze, however. "I guess that's part of the reason I was so embarrassed when I stared...for the first time...because, well...I thought you would think I was...just like *them*."

Cassie placed a hand on his cheek and turned his face toward her. "Adam...," she whispered, gazing longingly into his eyes, "you are nothing like them, and that's why I want to be with you."

Adam smiled, and Cassie couldn't hold back anymore. She threw her arms around him and kissed him passionately. To her delight, his lips responded in kind, and she pressed her hand to the back of his neck, pouring every ounce of passion within her into her kiss.

In that moment, all she wanted was him. Wrapped in his warm embrace, with their lips locked together in pure bliss, Cassie could think of nothing but him. If he would have laid her down and made love to her right then and there, she would have happily let him.

HOWEVER, IT WAS NOT to happen that night. After their usual parting, Cassie walked in her front door, still feeling exhilarated from the most intense make-out session of her life.

"Having a good time?"

Cassie's good mood evaporated immediately. *Kaleb.* "What's it to you?" she snapped.

He sat in the dining room, his clasped hands resting on the table. Thankfully, he wasn't looking at her. "Word gets around in this town, you know," Kaleb stated, still staring at his joined hands.

Cassie's eyes narrowed. *What is he up to?* "Your point?"

"Have you been meeting that boy of yours every Saturday?" he asked with an edge to his voice that took Cassie aback.

Tread carefully, Asmodeous warned.

"So what if I have?"

Kaleb looked up at her at last. "When were you planning on telling us this?"

Cassie's anger rose immediately. "I wasn't aware I was obligated to inform you of anything I do."

Kaleb stood up abruptly. "Excuse me, young lady? We are your parents!"

At those words, Cassie's anger boiled over. *Hurt him. Hurt him bad.* "My *parents*? *You* stopped being my 'parent' when you decided you wanted to fuck me!"

Kaleb's glare widened, and his hand resting on the table balled into a fist. "We adopted you, and that makes you our daughter!"

"Oh yeah? You've got a funny fucking way of showing it, you fucking pedophile!"

Stop this. Now.

Asmodeous's words tugged at Cassie's thoughts with an earnestness that caught her off guard, but her anger was in control. *I want him to hurt. He deserves to be hurt.*

"Don't talk to me like that! You still live in *our* house!"

"Because *I* told you to move here!"

"Irrelevant. It's our name on the mortgage. While you live in this house, you will abide by its rules."

"Does that mean I should strip down right now and let you have your way with me, then?"

Kaleb bared his teeth. "Stop. Bringing. That. Up."

Stop! Now!

But Cassie couldn't stop. She had him where she wanted him. The throbbing vein in his temple told her all she needed to know. She was pressing, he was squirming, and she loved it. "Tell that to your saggy cock the next time you..."

The next instant, Kaleb crossed the dining room and seized her by the scalp, tilting her head back. Cassie gasped in pain, and her body went rigid.

"Listen here, you little ungrateful..." but Kaleb's words cut off.

Cassie blinked and looked at him. His eyes slithered across her body, and his lips trembled over his clenched teeth. Whatever he was about to say had been forgotten. Cassie's anger immediately melted away, and pure terror took its place. *My god, he's about to rape me.*

"That will do," came her savior's voice out loud, and Cassie felt his presence erupt on the wall behind her.

Kaleb released her hair and backed away, his eyes bulging from their sockets when they locked on Asmodeous's shadowy form, now made visible. He shivered, and for a moment, his eyes shifted back to Cassie. His maddened gaze made Cassie want to cover her chest and abdomen in hopes it would somehow make her less appealing to him. However, he made no move toward her, as though Asmodeous's appearance was repelling him.

To your room and lock the door. Quickly.

Needing no second bidding, Cassie dashed down the hallway and slammed her door. She turned the lock and backed up to the post of her bed, shaking.

Asmodeous chastised, *I told you not to press him.*

Cassie grabbed her beloved cross-hilted dagger from her nightstand and sat on the bed, clutching it in white knuckles. *I...I wanted to hurt him.*

You were warned, but your feelings for this boy have made you reckless. Cassie winced, but before she could argue, Asmodeous continued. *Regardless, you must exercise greater caution.*

Cassie frowned. *You...You're not bothered by my feelings for Adam?*

Should I be? Are they endangering our plan?

Cassie bit her lip as her heart contracted. For a moment, she had considered revealing the plan to Adam, and that would have been nothing short of betrayal to Asmodeous. In the end, she had been unable to do it, but maybe Asmodeous knew that? Yet she couldn't deny that a very large part of her wanted to leave Adam out of it.

We are too close. It must be him.

Tears filled Cassie's eyes, but she nodded. *As you say, but...can I please just have a little more time with him? Please?*

Asmodeous was silent for a moment, but Cassie waited, trembling. Finally, he whispered, *You have until the Halloween party. Make the most of the time you have left.*

"Thank you so much," Cassie whispered aloud, joyful tears slipping down her cheeks. That left her with a little more than a month with Adam, and she intended to savor every sweet second with him until then. Her grip on the dagger relaxed, but then she remembered why she was holding it and looked at it. It was a simple weapon but beautiful in its deadliness. For a moment, she imagined driving it into Kaleb's neck. *I fucking hate him.*

Fear not. Once this stage of the plan is complete, he will be disposed of.

I hope I'm there to see it, Cassie thought with savage pleasure.

9. A Night to Remember

A month later, Halloween night arrived, and with it Adam's Halloween party. Adam woke up early that Saturday to prepare both the trail and the barn for the night's festivities before helping his mom decorate the house. As dusk began to fall, Adam was setting the dining room table for the snack trays and various other refreshments when Ken's car pulled into the driveway.

Grinning with anticipation for the night to come, Adam called to his mom in the kitchen, "The guys are here, Mom. I'm gonna get them set up."

"Is the table ready?" she asked in reply.

Adam surveyed the dining room. Spiderweb tablecloth? Check. Skull candelabra? Check. Paper plate stack, napkins, and plastic utensils? Check, check, check. Satisfied, he replied, "Yep!"

"Then consider yourself relieved of your decorating duties!"

"Roger!" Adam answered, heading outside to greet his friends.

The four of them got out of the car and headed Adam's way. Their costumes waited inside the barn in the back yard.

Adam grinned. "Barn is all set up, so just head on in!"

Damien touched two fingers to his brow in salute, shouldering a backpack, and headed toward the barn. Lex nodded with a satisfied smile and followed suit. Walter was nearly shaking with excitement as he brought up the rear. "This is gonna be sweet!"

Ken got out last and hung back as the others walked away. "I think he's more excited than the rest of you guys combined."

Adam laughed. "Nah, he's just worse at hiding it."

"Is Cassie gonna be here?"

Adam's heart leapt. "Yep!"

"Need help setting up anything?"

Adam shook his head. "Already done for the most part. I will need a little help directing traffic, though, once people start arriving."

Ken nodded. "Not a problem. Where do you want me?"

Adam shrugged. "Wherever the people are, I guess?"

Ken chuckled and shook his head. "As you say, mon capitaine." He headed into the house.

Adam chewed his lip for a moment, unsure of what to do next. The walk was prepped, the food area was set, and his friends were all getting ready. All that was left for him to do was to wait.

Guests began arriving a short while later. Word must have gotten around because a lot more people showed up than Adam had ever hosted before. He greeted them all in turn, but his mind was on Cassie. Was she not going to show up? She was usually early for their meetups in the woods, so why would she be late to the party? As more people arrived, he found it harder and harder to hide his agitation.

At last, Cassie arrived a half hour into the party, dropped off by a balding old man Adam assumed was her father. She climbed out of the car and brushed off her long, black trench coat before turning to smile at Adam. Her smile revealed a pair of plastic fangs; she was dressed as a vampiress. Cassie had also put on a thick layer of eye shadow around her eyes, perhaps to make them appear sunken or deathly, but instead, it made her crystal blue eyes pop in a way that delighted Adam. The goth look suited her well.

The partygoers were gathered in the front and back yard, enjoying refreshments. Those in the front yard fell silent when Cassie sauntered over to Adam and kissed his cheek.

"How do I look?" Despite the fangs, she spoke astonishingly clearly.

"You look great," Adam said, blushing furiously.

Cassie smiled and took his arm. "So, what's the plan for festivities tonight?"

Adam placed a hand over hers. "In about a half-hour, I have to get ready."

"Oh?"

Adam grinned mischievously and whispered, "Ken is gonna take guests on a walk around the property. Me and the others are gonna have a few surprises for them."

Cassie giggled. "That's gonna be awesome!"

"Don't tell anyone, though," Adam cautioned.

"I don't talk to anyone but you and the guys anyways."

"Speaking of which…" Adam looked at her with curiosity. "How are you still sounding so normal with the teeth in?"

Cassie giggled and popped one of the fangs off of her canine. "It's a special type. Designed to look and feel more natural than the toy veneers most vampire makeup kits come with."

"Impressive," Adam admitted, nodding in approval.

"Figured I should go the extra mile for the occasion."

"Which reminds me," Adam said, "there's someone you need to meet."

"Lead the way." Cassie gave his arm a gentle squeeze.

Adam took Cassie inside, his stomach in knots. He had told his parents about Cassie only a few weeks ago, and his mother had demanded to meet her for herself. Adam had warned Cassie about this at school, but she didn't seem bothered.

As they headed for the kitchen where his mother was putting the finishing touches on a second bowl of her ever-popular taco salad, Cassie looked more at ease than Adam felt.

"Hey, Mom?" Adam called.

"Yes?" She churned the contents of a salad bowl with a large spoon, focused on her work.

Adam swallowed nervously. "This...is Cassie."

His mom stopped her work and turned to face them both. She looked Cassie up and down, and Adam held his breath. She offered her hand. "I'm Adam's mom, in case that wasn't obvious."

Cassie smiled and took her hand. "Glad to meet you."

"Adam said you moved from Valpo?"

Cassie nodded. "Yep, just at the beginning of the school year."

"How are you liking the smaller town?"

Cassie shrugged. "It's definitely safer. That's the biggest reason we moved. It's nice to be able to walk around without getting nervous."

"You live in town, then?"

"Yep, just on the other side of the woods from the school."

Adam's mom nodded in approval before turning back to her work. "I better get this together. These kids can't seem to get enough. Nice meeting you!"

"You too!" Cassie replied cheerfully before she and Adam headed back out into the yard.

Relief washed over Adam. From what he could tell, it had gone well. Cassie had been perfectly personable, and his mom had seemed content with the girl's answers to her questions. He doubted they'd heard the last of them, but at least things were off to a good start.

Adam heaved a sigh. "Well, I suppose I better make sure everyone's enjoying themselves. Gotta be a good host and all." He offered his arm to Cassie. "Shall we?"

Cassie giggled and took it once again. "But of course!"

They headed out the front door, finding a trio of girls at the porch swing. First among them was Kelsey. She had gone all out for her costume with a floral kimono, geisha makeup, and a paper fan. Kelsey was a little broader than Cassie but about the same height, and her light brown hair had been sprayed black and done up in a bun held together by a pair of chopsticks. She had been talking to her friends Jessica and Samantha before Adam and Cassie walked up but fell silent as they approached.

"Hey guys!" Jessica greeted them cheerfully. She was both taller and broader than Kelsey, with her dark hair back in a ponytail. She was dressed in a maid's outfit with cat ears and makeup whiskers to match.

"How are you guys doing? Need anything?" Adam asked politely.

"All good here!" Jessica replied.

Samantha simply shook her head. Unlike her two companions, she hadn't dressed up for the night. She was the leanest of the three. Her dark hair was half-up and half-down, and she wore a pair of wire-frame glasses. Samantha's outfit was the same as what she wore to school every day: a zip-up hooded sweatshirt, a rock band T-shirt, and a worn-out pair of blue jeans.

"I'm curious," Kelsey asked. "How did you two meet anyways?"

Adam almost rolled his eyes. He should have expected this.

Before he could even debate on how to answer her question however, Cassie replied, "He caught up to me while I was walking home from school, and we just sort of hit it off."

Jessica shot Kelsey a scolding look from the corner of her eye, but Kelsey ignored her. "What do you guys do together? Like, for fun and stuff?"

"Just hang out," Adam said simply.

"Just hang out?" Kelsey repeated skeptically.

"Yep, that's all really," Cassie added with a flip of her hair.

Adam had to fight the urge to grin like a fool. *She's teasing her.*

Kelsey then asked, "So how far have you guys—"

"Hey, Adam!" Jessica interjected. "Don't you want to check on the rest of your guests?"

Adam chuckled. "Right! Better get on that. Have fun, you guys!" As he and Cassie walked past a very huffy-looking Kelsey, Adam almost laughed out loud. *We're gonna have her in tears later.*

Once they were out of earshot, Cassie whispered, "Holy fuck, she's nosy!"

"I know," Adam agreed. "She's kind of the class gossip."

Cassie giggled. "No subtlety there."

Adam chuckled lightly as they rounded the corner of the house to the back yard, where they found a small group of marching band kids gathered in a loose circle. Among them was Taylor Bronson, Adam's former crush. They approached the group, while Taylor recounted an incident from a recent marching competition.

"So there we are, waiting for them to call us back for line-up, and Jake comes over and is like, 'Hey, let's tune!' So my dumbass is about to play a tone before he *politely* reminds me that we're not supposed to play until we're in the warmup area!"

A tall, broad boy with a blond buzz cut named Tony laughed aloud, his back to Adam and Cassie. He hadn't dressed up, but Adam wasn't surprised. Tony's casual shorts and T-shirt getup was his signature look.

"I can't believe you fell for it! That's almost as bad as when I tripped over my own feet at step-off when we took the field. You little horns can get away with it, but when you're toting those big-ass sousaphones..." His story earned a chuckle from the group.

"Hey," Adam interjected, "sorry to interrupt, but I just wanted to see if you guys needed anything."

The circle turned to look at him with several assurances that they were doing just fine, but then Taylor stepped forward from the group. She was not much shorter than Cassie, dressed in a violet corseted dress and a black velvet cloak. Her light brown and wavy hair was half-up and half-down, and her hazel eyes and round face were lit up with a friendly smile. "Actually, I need to meet your girlfriend!"

This could get awkward. Adam tried not to show his nerves. "Well, here she is. Cassie, this is Taylor. Taylor, Cassie."

Cassie stepped forward and shook Taylor's outstretched hand. "Good to meet you."

"I've wanted to talk to you for forever, but you always look like you don't want to be bothered at school."

Cassie shrugged. "I've never been good at socializing."

Taylor nodded knowingly. "I get it. Still, we should talk some time!" She paused a moment, taking in Cassie's outfit properly, then giggled. "I'm sorry, but I just gotta say, you're just so pretty! You really need to dress like this more often. It really suits you!"

To Adam's surprise, Cassie smiled, her cheeks flushing only slightly. "Thanks."

Taylor grinned. "Adam is a really lucky guy, honestly."

"Yeah, now that he's off *her* back," came a mumble from the circle.

Taylor glared over her shoulder at the speaker—Jake, the trombone player. He was a short boy with an oval-shaped face, rounded cheeks, and short, dark hair. He, too, was dressed casually, though his cargo pants and T-shirt must have been a size too big for how loosely they hung on him.

Taylor blushed slightly and snapped, "It's not like that, and you know it!"

Silence hung over the group for a second before Taylor turned back to face them and offered an apologetic smile.

"Sorry about that. Umm...Cassie, can I talk to you alone for a second?"

Cassie looked at Adam. His stomach was restless, but Taylor was not known for being malicious. Despite his nerves, he nodded.

"Go ahead, it's fine."

With another apologetic smile for Adam, Taylor and Cassie stepped off to the side and out of earshot of the group.

Tony turned to face Jake. "Seriously, dude, that was not cool."

"Yeah, kind of a dick thing to say," a tall, lanky, black-haired trumpet player named Drew added. He was decked out in a mad scientist outfit, complete with a pocket full of test tubes and a fictional lab corporation's emblem on the breast.

Jake held up his hands in apology. "I'm sorry, dude! It just kinda...slipped out." He turned to face Adam. "We cool?"

Adam almost smirked, thinking of how he'd have his own form of revenge soon that very night. Instead, he smiled. "Yeah, we're cool. No harm, no foul."

Tony chuckled. "You're a hell of a lot nicer than me, man."

Adam grinned, his mind on the surprise to come. *Just wait.* Moments later, Cassie and Taylor came back to the group, both smiling.

Adam asked, "All good, ladies?"

Cassie nodded, and Taylor smiled before turning back to her. "We'll talk more later, okay?"

Cassie grinned in return. "Sure thing!" She took Adam's arm once more, and they headed off to check on the other guests.

As they walked, Adam asked, "So how'd your chat go?"

Cassie shrugged. "She just said she didn't want any bad blood between us. She'd known you'd had a crush on her for years, and she always felt bad about not feeling the same. She said you deserved something real. She honestly seems to think pretty highly of you."

Adam blushed. "She's always been nice to me, at least."

Cassie giggled. "I can see why you'd have a crush on her, though. She's sweet...and she's pretty cute."

Adam chuckled, relieved things had gone well enough. Maybe Cassie having a female friend would be good for her. Then he checked his watch. It was nearly time. Adam turned to Cassie. "Gotta go get ready now. Want to come with?"

Cassie giggled excitedly but said, "No thanks, I wanna see the show from the audience's perspective."

"You'll be all right on your own for a bit?" Cassie nodded with a smile, and Adam grinned. "I hope you like it."

"I'm sure I will," Cassie cooed before kissing Adam on the cheek.

Adam headed for the barn in the far corner of the backyard. After checking to make sure no one was watching, he slipped inside through the side door. The barn was usually empty, but tonight it was their base of operations. A handful of menacing hand props, several costume pieces, and Adam's friends were scattered about.

Walter was already dressed up in his skeletal cowboy outfit. When Adam arrived, his friend held up a small cap gun and asked, "How's this for a little oomph to my act?"

Adam chuckled and gave him a thumbs-up. "Good idea!"

Damien wore a black hood that hid his face with a pair of large, glowing red eyes. His black clothes were covered in chains, and he looked intimidating.

Lex sat holding his burlap sack mask, dressed in a bloodied apron, waiting for the time to arrive.

Adam crossed the barn, finding his own costume in a pile on an old wooden table. He donned black robes with skull embroidery and a black hooded cloak. Adam then slipped on a pair of black gloves and a metallic, fanged skull mask. Finally, he grabbed a gargoyle-topped staff from the corner.

"So now we wait for the signal from Ken," Damien stated.

"Yep, now we wait," Lex agreed.

"That mask staying on?" Adam asked Walter.

Walter turned to face him, running his fingers along the edge of his skull mask. "Doesn't feel like it's peeling off."

"Someday we should find something better than spirit gum," Lex said.

"Someday," Adam agreed, and then his phone vibrated in his pocket. He pulled his robes up to grab it and made sure that it was Ken, giving them the all-clear. He was not disappointed. "Time to move. Everyone remember their spots?"

The whole crew nodded. Lex pulled his burlap sack over his head. He had crudely painted a red grin and blackened eyes onto it. Lex grabbed a chainless chainsaw from the floor in front of him. The other two were already on their feet and ready to move.

Brimming with excitement, Adam peeked out of the side door of the barn. As planned, the crowd had disappeared to follow Ken. With the coast clear, Adam waved his friends onward, and the gang dispersed into the woods and field on the west side of Adam's family's property. Lex was to be the grand finale closest to the house, with Adam preceding him. Damien would be the guests' first encounter, followed closely by Walter.

While Adam waited, he checked the power cords to his lights and speakers. Everything was in perfect working order. Then he heard the screams as Damien roared menacingly. Adrenaline poured into Adam's blood; he lived for this. He took position in the trees, hearing Walter's cap gun go off, followed swiftly by more screams and some good-hearted laughter. Adam closed his eyes, letting his hearing tell him all he needed to know, while he focused on what came next. His mind was blissfully blank, his muscles coiled like a cat ready to pounce. His free hand opened and closed, and anticipation built inside him.

Then the guests rounded the edge of the tree line where he had hidden. *Not yet.* Timing was everything. The group proceeded slowly. Adam was unable to distinguish faces through the black cloth over the eyes of his mask, but it hardly mattered. He breathed slowly as the group meandered by, waiting for the central mass of people to fall directly in front of him. When at last he saw what he was waiting for, Adam placed one foot on a pressure plate hidden in the tall grass before striding out with his arms spread and his staff raised. A fan started in the trees, causing his robes to billow dramatically. A light flashed like lightning, and the concealed speakers boomed thunder and howling wind. With a growling, monstrous voice, Adam declared, "Unwelcome ones, your time has come!"

The guests were in awe of his antics. A few stopped to stare at him, and he brought the staff down to the ground in time with another flash of light. The group moved along, with Adam cackling maniacally in his diabolic voice. He felt empowered, like a god before mere mortals. Adrenaline still chased through his system, ignited anew as soon as Lex's chainsaw roared to life and more screams erupted. Adam didn't care that his performance didn't get many scares. Their awe was just as intoxicating as the screams of terror.

Walter and Damien came up behind him. "That was awesome!" Walter exclaimed.

"I think I made someone piss themselves," Damien said with a laugh.

"We're not done yet," Adam replied with a wicked grin beneath his mask. "Let's get 'em again!"

With roars of agreement, the three of them raced after the guests, diving among them with Lex, scattering them all throughout the yard. It finally ended when the four of them fell to the ground, laughing.

Ken walked up to them, shaking his head and grinning from ear to ear. "Someday, I may decide to switch places with one of you."

"Better yet, just find a replacement," Adam said, chuckling. He climbed back to his feet and pulled off his mask. The guests applauded, and his eyes went wide. "Well, that's new."

Ken said, "They loved it. You outdid yourself this year."

Adam flushed a little but smiled broadly. "I love Halloween."

"We know." Walter threw an arm around him.

"Now it's our turn to party!" Damien declared, pulling his red-eyed mask off.

The party went on for some time after. Adam's hidden stereo played music while everyone danced, mingled, ate, or played video games in the living room. Adam had kept his costume on, enjoying himself too much to think of taking it off.

Finally, Cassie caught up to him. "Adam, that was amazing."

"Did you really think so?"

"It was," Cassie assured him. "Wanna go for a walk? I'm not so big on the crowds…"

"Me either," Adam agreed. "Any particular destination in mind?"

"Follow me," Cassie said with a fanged grin.

How does she make those look so natural?

The pair slipped away from the party, into the trees, and onto the path the group had followed earlier. Cassie took him to a secluded spot near the very edge of the property, then turned to him.

"You were absolutely fantastic tonight."

"Could you tell who I was?" Adam asked, still grinning.

"Actually, yes," Cassie said with a wink. "Your act was very dynamic. Powerful, even." She looked at the ground. "I have to admit…" Her eyes shifted up to face him as she whispered, "It turned me on."

Adam's breath caught in his throat. The look she had given him, the full moon illuminating her pale skin, made his blood race.

Cassie stepped forward, slipped her arms around him, and whispered in his ear, "I want you."

Adam shuddered involuntarily before she pressed her lips to his. She kissed him hungrily, without hesitation or restraint. Adam forgot everything else from earlier that night. His only thoughts were her sweet breath in his mouth and her tongue caressing his own. The night had already been warm, but suddenly, it seemed far warmer. Hot, even.

Cassie stepped back and unbuttoned her coat, her eyes locked on him. Adam hesitated for a moment, struggling to keep his thoughts clear. *Should we?* She must have noticed, for she paused and looked at him, her eyes smoldering.

"Something wrong?"

Adam bit his lip. *Yes, you are too beautiful to want me. This is a dream, and you are perfect, and God, I'm in love with you.* His thoughts danced around before he finally whispered, "I...I don't want to lose you."

Cassie's lips turned up in a sultry smile. "You won't. I promise."

Adam might have protested further, but then the coat was off. Cassie had gotten bolder with her clothes the more time they had spent together, but nothing could have prepared him for the black corset and mini skirt she was hiding under the coat. Her outfit was both elegant and sensual, overwhelming Adam's senses with a desire he couldn't have resisted, even if he wanted to.

Within moments, all thought was entirely impossible. There was only that moment, the warm air around them, and her, a goddess given form. He was hers.

10. The Girl Alone

Cassie's mind was pure bliss. Whatever she had expected her first time to feel like, it hadn't been that. Adam had let her take the lead from the start, and she had run with it. She was still trembling, even as she lay next to him, her coat between them and the ground and his robe as a blanket draped over them. Cassie gently stroked his chest with her fingertips, feeling an odd sensation of both peace and exhilaration. His eyes were closed, his arms were around her, and nothing was between them but the night. If they could lie there together forever, Cassie would be content.

Cassandra.

A part of Cassie had known it was coming, but that didn't stop her chest from tightening when Asmodeous's voice interrupted her thoughts.

Remember your purpose.

Cassie bit her lip, trying with all of her might not to let tears fill her eyes, lest it disturb Adam from whatever he was thinking about behind those closed eyes and that contented smile. For only the second time in thirteen years, she considered betraying Asmodeous, but as before, she couldn't do it. Even as she looked up at the face of the boy she had fallen in love with, she couldn't turn her back on the one who had raised her after her real parents had died. Still, the thought of what she was about to do was tearing away at her. Cassie took a deep, shaky breath. *Please...can I keep him...just a little longer?*

The more time you have with him, the more you will crave.

Cassie thought about Asmodeous's response. Maybe just another few months? Spending the summer together in the grove. Graduating together. She even almost giggled at the idea of jumping into his arms for a photo op in their caps and gowns. Maybe then she'd be ready, but the aisle of graduation in her mind's eye shifted to the aisle of a church, and there was a bouquet in her hands as she walked up to a slightly older Adam in a tuxedo. His eyes glistened with joyful tears, and his lips turned up in a smile Cassie knew couldn't do justice to the happiness overflowing from both of them. They would be together forever...

But there was truth behind Asmodeous's words. She would never be ready to let Adam go. The longer things went on between them, the more she dreaded what she and Asmodeous had planned for him, and the worse it would get. She could only see herself falling more in love with Adam, until perhaps one day she found the courage to choose him over her shadow, the one who had protected her from horrors unimaginable.

It must be now.

I know, Cassie thought solemnly. She was out of time, and nothing could prevent the tears slipping from her eyes.

Take heart; it will not be permanent.

Cassie paused. *What do you mean?*

Once my purpose is complete, I will no longer need him. I can return him to you then.

Cassie's heart leapt. *You mean it?*

You have my word.

Cassie looked up at Adam once again. It was cold comfort but comfort nonetheless. Emboldened by Asmodeous's promise, Cassie set her mind to the task at hand. She feigned stretching, her hand sifting through the pile of her clothes. Just inside her trench coat was a pocket containing a small razor blade. She gingerly pulled the blade out and shifted her position next to Adam. Nervously, she glanced up at his face. His eyes were still closed. Cassie froze, her resolve shaken as affection surged through her. Through gritted teeth and with fresh tears in her eyes that had nothing to do with physical pain, she ran the blade across her forearm pinned against Adam, inflicting a small cut on herself that welled up with blood immediately.

After tossing the blade back to her clothes pile, Cassie gently ran her fingers along the wound. *Remember the symbols.* After checking once more to make sure Adam was oblivious, she gently drew a series of symbols in her blood over his heart. The going was slow, and she needed to refresh the blood on her fingertips several times before the sigil was complete. *Patience. Always patience.* Adam was lost in ignorant bliss. If his breathing were only a little shallower, Cassie would have thought he had fallen asleep.

Finally, Cassie traced the last rune. The moment her fingertip left Adam's chest, a chill descended on her back. *This is it.* Her shadow pulled itself from the grass around them and loomed over Adam. As he had appeared in all of Cassie's dreams, her protector was little more than a hooded and cloaked figure...but not for long. The shadow condensed into a cloud of black smoke. It lingered over Adam for a moment before rushing into the runes on his chest. The chill that had enveloped them was gone. The sigil glowed violet for a moment, then faded entirely, and Adam's body went completely limp.

I did it. When Cassie had imagined this moment a hundred times before, she had expected to feel triumphant. Now that it was done, however, all she felt was shame.

Her heart heavy, Cassie closed her eyes and savored what might be the last time she could lay her head on Adam's chest. *Please forgive me, my love...*

CASSIE DIDN'T BOTHER keeping track of how long she lay next to Adam's unconscious body. She let herself cry freely and stroked his chest once more, as though she might undo what had been done. There was no going back, but that didn't stop Cassie from longing for earlier that night.

When Adam began to stir, Cassie held her breath, her mind suddenly blank. She had no idea what to expect. Adam's face tightened for a moment before his eyes blinked open, and he looked down at her. Cassie's heart did cartwheels in her chest—the same brown eyes he had always had. Her face lit up in a delighted smile, and her joy welled over. Adam blinked again.

"I...I guess I dozed off."

Cassie wanted to tell him that it was all right, but her feelings overwhelmed her. Unable to speak at all, she threw herself onto his lips and kissed him with everything she had. Her passion reignited, and she gave herself to him once again with complete abandon.

THE PARTY WAS WINDING down. Many of the guests had left, though enough remained for Adam and Cassie's absence to go unnoticed. Cassie wasn't sure how long they had been gone, but it hardly mattered. For now, she still had Adam for herself, and she intended to make the most of whatever time he had left before Asmodeous took over.

Adam sat down on the couch in the living room, and Cassie sat beside him, laying her head on his shoulder while his friends launched into their usual virtual rivalries. While Adam stroked her hair, she thought of Asmodeous.

Are you there?

There was no reply. With a soft sigh, Cassie went over the events of the evening in her mind. Making love to Adam had been heavenly, and even more so the second time. She also felt a degree of exaltation from fulfilling her promise to Asmodeous, despite her fears and trepidations. But even as she sat next to Adam, surrounded by his friends, she imagined making love to him again and again. *This could be a problem.*

Around midnight, Cassie realized that she had a different dilemma. She sat up and stretched before saying, "I'm gonna need a ride home. I don't think your parents will let me stay with you all."

"I can give you a lift," Ken volunteered.

Cassie finished stretching. "Sounds good." She turned to Adam and hugged him. "I had a wonderful time tonight."

Adam hugged her tightly and whispered in her ear, "Me too."

Cassie shuddered slightly with delight and kissed his cheek. "Until next time." She stood up, said goodbye to the others, and walked out with Ken. Without another word, they got into Ken's car and left.

"So," Ken began as they pulled out of Adam's driveway, "did you have fun tonight?"

"Yes," Cassie said simply, suddenly aware of how alone she was with him. Something about her answer must have put him off, however. Most of the rest of the ride to her house was in silence. Cassie stared out the window, a hollow feeling creeping into her chest. She was alone. Completely. The idea of going home so alone made her shiver in fear. She asked Ken, "Could you drop me off at the edge of the woods, by the school?"

Ken frowned. "Are you sure? It's pretty late."

"I'm sure."

"All right," Ken said with skepticism. Without any other comment, he drove her down the streets to the cafeteria parking lot. He put the car in park and turned to face her, his expression stern. "You know, Adam's a very nice guy," he said.

"I know," Cassie replied simply, unsure of what was about to happen.

Ken's eyes met hers. His stare was hard and scrutinizing. "Please don't hurt him."

Whatever Cassie had been prepared to hear, it hadn't been that. *Is that all?* She met his gaze and answered confidently, "I won't."

"Good," Ken said simply. He called, "Good night!" to her as she climbed out of the car.

Cassie didn't reply. She started toward the woods until Ken drove off. With no one left around to see her, she broke into a run. Cassie raced through the woods until she came to her grove. The moonlight illuminated it like a pale spotlight. She didn't want to go home, not without Asmodeous. The thought of what Kaleb might do to her without him there made her skin crawl. Instead, she climbed the tree and positioned herself in her favorite seat, leaning back to look up at the moon.

Cassie didn't know how long she lay on the tree before she realized she was crying. She sat up and wiped her eyes, wondering what had made her tear up. Then she knew: she missed Asmodeous. His absence had left an emptiness in her chest that was slowly growing. She recalled all the times he protected her, from the moment Kaleb came to her in the night to scaring off a man with a knife in the city, to keeping her one step ahead of the gang of would-be rapists as they tried to attack her. Cassie also thought of when he had walked with her out of the cellar of Corbant Manor, where her entire family had been slaughtered.

A chill rose in the night, stirring Cassie from her perch. The air was growing heavy, threatening rain. Reluctantly, she started home. *At least Kaleb won't know he's gone. How long could it last, though?* She had never felt so alone in the entirety of her life.

The walk to her house was agonizingly long and slow. With as much stealth as she could muster, she unlocked the door and crept in. Once inside, she took off her boots and held them as she snuck to her bedroom. Every shadow around her threatened to conceal Kaleb or any of the other men who had lusted for her. Every glimmer of light resembled the edge of a blade to be used to threaten her. Cassie's fear goaded her to move faster until, at last, she was behind her locked bedroom door.

Cassie pressed her back against it, fresh tears rolling down her cheeks. In the safety of her room, only the emptiness remained.

She slid down to the floor and hugged her knees as she cried. Though she had known this was coming all along, the sudden loss of her closest friend and protector was crushing. She wanted him back. Cassie wanted to feel his presence around her and hear his voice in her head. She missed the one who had lived in her shadow for thirteen years.

Cassie eventually crawled into bed, not bothering to remove any of her clothing. The idea of exposing herself, even for a second, made her stomach turn over. She pulled the covers up to her chin and rolled to her side, a fresh wave of despair sweeping over her. The hollow feeling in her chest was all she knew now. *I hate this...I hate this so much.*

Cassie sobbed quietly in the dark, clutching the blanket to her chest. Asmodeous had done so much for her, and now he was gone. She was lost and scared, suddenly alone in a vast, cruel world. To make matters worse, she had consigned the love of her life to what could be a fate worse than death. Loneliness and self-loathing for her betrayal left Cassie curling into a ball, crying aloud.

As she closed her eyes, she whispered, "Please...forgive me...my love..." Fresh sobs overtook her, and she eventually cried herself to sleep.

11. Bad News

Adam awoke with a start. The sun shone brightly through the blinds of his upstairs bedroom. Puzzled, Adam looked at the clock on the headboard. The time read 1:09 p.m. Shaking his head, Adam tried to recall the last details of the night before. He remembered falling asleep on the couch after Cassie left, but nothing after that. Adam didn't even remember changing into his pajama pants, but he felt their familiar texture against his legs instead of his usual jeans.

He sat up slowly as footsteps came up the stairs. He looked out his open door, finding his mother approaching. She offered him a weak smile.

"About time you're awake."

"Did everyone leave already?" Adam asked with a yawn.

"Three hours ago. You slept like the dead."

Adam blinked and shook his head slightly. Oversleeping always left him with an annoying headache. He was about to ask what she wanted when he heard his father, Ray, coming up the stairs. His dad was only slightly taller than him, with short, dark hair peppered with gray and a bushy mustache of the same color. He wore a simple sweatshirt featuring a wintry painting along with faded blue jeans that had seen far better years.

His dad took a deep breath before stating firmly, "We need to talk."

Adam tried to hide the nerves that rose within him instantly at those words. Had they somehow found out about him and Cassie last night? However, his fears were immediately replaced when his mother said with tears in her eyes, "Your grandma is in the hospital."

"What? What happened?" Adam asked, his mind suddenly very numb.

"She had a stroke," his dad replied, "and things aren't looking very good."

"Is she...?" Adam began, unwilling to say any more.

"Not yet," his dad answered, and his mom buried her face in his dad's shoulder. "Evey is there with her right now. She went in just this morning."

"Evey's there too?" Adam asked.

His dad nodded. "She's gonna need someone to look after her while Grandma's in the hospital. We've volunteered to do that, but we're gonna need some help. She can't be left alone," his dad warned.

"I know." Adam climbed out of bed.

"That means on Saturdays, you'll need to stay home until one of us gets home to watch her."

A strange numbness settled over Adam. "I understand."

"We were going to go get her after we told you what happened. Wanna come with?" his mother asked, finally pulling her tear-stained face out of her husband's side.

"Of course," Adam answered, going to his dresser to get his clothes.

Corbanton had no hospital of its own. Instead, they went to the next city over, where Adam's grandmother was being kept. On the ride there, Adam thought about how Evey living with them would change things. His heart ached for the poor girl. She had lived with his grandmother for two years now, and it had helped improve her condition. Their grandmother was a kindly, soft-spoken woman of seventy-nine years and was the perfect caretaker for little Evey.

Adam milled over all his memories with both Evey and his grandmother, even as they entered the hospital and took the elevator to her floor. Though he hated to admit it, Adam was already preparing himself for his grandmother's death. A stroke had taken his grandfather eight years ago, and this situation felt far too similar.

They entered the ward and found a pair of nurses tending to his grandmother. Little Evey sat in a chair nearby.

His grandmother was thin and frail, with her mouth hanging slightly open and her lips sunken. Her eyes were closed as if in slumber, and her short hair was white and curly. Her hands were bent in on themselves and unmoving. The nurses addressed his parents as they came in, but Adam went to Evey and kneeled in front of her.

"Hello, Evey."

She squeaked, "A. K.!" and jumped out of her chair to throw her arms around Adam's neck.

"Nice to see you too, Evey," he whispered in her ear, hugging her back.

Evey pulled away and looked at him, grinning with her soft, brown eyes alight. She glanced over Adam's shoulder, and her expression grew puzzled. "Why is your shadow so weird?"

"What do you mean?" Adam asked with a slight chuckle.

"It looks...different," Evey said, frowning.

Adam glanced over his shoulder. The dim lighting in the room had turned his shadow on the wall to his left into a vague blur, but nothing seemed out of the ordinary about it. Adam turned to look back at her and said, "I don't see anything wrong with it. Have you taken your meds this morning?"

Evey nodded vigorously. "Mhm! The nurse helped me figure everything out."

"That's good," Adam said, though there was an odd sense of dread at Evey's observation. He brushed the feeling away. "So you know you're going to come live with us for a while, right?"

"I am?" Evey tittered excitedly.

"Just until Grandma gets better," Adam assured her, ignoring the stabbing pain in his chest at the lie.

"Will that be soon, A. K.?" Evey asked innocently, though her eyes betrayed a hint of worry he understood all too well.

Adam fought tears for a moment. "I hope so." He looked at his grandmother once again. His mother was holding her hand, crying silently, while his dad talked to the doctor outside.

This is unfair.

Adam looked around in confusion. The voice had seemingly come from nowhere. No one else was in the room besides himself, Evey, his mother, and grandmother, and it assuredly had not been a woman's voice.

Adam wondered for a moment if Evey's question about his shadow and the phantom voice were connected but dismissed it. He had enough to worry about now without jumping at oddities.

THE RIDE HOME FELT shorter than the ride to the hospital. Adam's mom explained to Evey how things would work from now on. Evey assured them all it would not be terribly different from what she was accustomed to. She would catch the bus in the morning with Adam, then ride home with him at the end of the day. Evey would be staying in the guest bedroom directly opposite Adam's on the upstairs landing. They assured her that if she had any problems to come and find one of them immediately. Evey obediently agreed, then hummed to herself as she watched the world zoom by the car window.

Meanwhile, Adam finally took a moment to think about how things would change now that Evey was living with them. He was certain that either his friends wouldn't be allowed over at all or at least not in big groups. The high energy and good-natured banter might prove too overwhelming for Evey's delicate mental state.

Adam also wondered if he would be able to continue his training lessons with Cassie on Saturdays. His mother would usually get home between 3:30 and 5:00 p.m., depending on how busy the post office was. With that level of uncertainty as to when he could leave the house, Adam wasn't sure it would be possible to maintain their arrangement. However, he'd save discussing that with Cassie until Monday, while he helped Evey get settled in.

The remainder of the day, Adam and his dad collected Evey's things from his grandmother's house and brought them home, while his mom stayed with Evey. By the day's end, Adam was thoroughly exhausted. He expected to fall asleep the moment his head hit the pillow that night, but it was not to be a restful experience.

Adam dreamt he was back in the hospital room with his grandmother. The doctor leaned over her, his face obscured by a surgeon's mask. He stood up and pulled the mask off, revealing the face of Adam's grandfather, who said in the same voice Adam had heard earlier that afternoon, "This is unfair."

Evey jumped up from her chair and ran to hug Adam's waist, then leaned back and asked, "A. K., why is your shadow so scary?"

"This is unfair," the voice repeated, this time from no visible source. It filled the room, and Adam glanced over his shoulder, seeing not his own shadow, but the shadow of a cloaked figure. "This is unfair," it repeated. The shadow grew, slowly engulfing the entire wall and ceiling. Soon, the voice grew louder, repeating again and again, "This is unfair. This is unfair."

The shadow extended until all the walls and everything on them were covered by a thin veil of darkness. Adam turned back toward Evey and his grandmother. The voice boomed in his ears, and the color drained from their flesh. To Adam's horror, their skin began to melt away, revealing the bones beneath. The voice continued to scream, *"This is unfair!"* Adam might have been screaming, too, but he couldn't hear over the voice repeating, *"This is unfair!"*

Adam sat bolt upright in his bed, bathed in cold sweat. He looked around the darkness of his room frantically, taking a moment to remember he was at home and not in the hospital anymore. He placed a hand to his chest as if to steady his racing heart. If not for the voice still ringing in his ears, he might have noticed that his alarm for school was going off. When it finally dawned on him what time it was, he went into Evey's room to wake her, dragging his feet from exhaustion. He felt as though he hadn't gotten any sleep whatsoever the night before. He gave Evey a gentle shake.

"Time to get up, Evey."

"Unfair!" Evey squeaked. As she sprang up, her eyes rolled back for a moment.

Adam's heart froze. All tiredness left him immediately, and he tensed up as he asked, "What...What's unfair?"

"What are you talking about, A. K.?" she said, looking at him.

Adam frowned. "You just said 'unfair.'"

"No, I didn't. Is it time for school?" Evey asked, seemingly oblivious.

"I...well...yeah, time to get ready," Adam replied, dumbstruck.

"Okay!" Evey exclaimed cheerfully, hopping out of bed, leaving him both confused and disturbed.

As Adam's adrenaline from Evey's outburst began to fade, his exhaustion crept back up on him. His eyelids grew heavier, waiting for the bus at the end of the driveway. He struggled to stay awake on the bus while Evey stared out the window quietly, kicking her legs beneath the seat. With the fear of the dream gone from his mind, all that remained was the sorrow for his grandmother, and Adam could not hope to fight it off, being as tired as he was.

Far too soon for Adam's liking, they arrived at the high school. Evey hugged him and said, "Have a good day, A. K.!"

"I'll try, Evey." Adam hugged her back with one arm, then made his way off the bus, leaving Evey with the rest of the middle and elementary school kids. Adam felt as though he were on autopilot from the cafeteria doors to his locker and finally to the couches, where his friends waited. Whether it was his exhaustion or his depression that showed on his face, they were quick to notice.

Damien asked, concerned, "What's wrong, Adam?"

"I…" Adam hesitated, not really desiring the sympathy he knew he'd receive, but it seemed unfair not to tell his friends at least most of what was bothering him. "I wanna wait for Cassie, then I'll tell you."

"All right," Damien said nervously.

The group was uncharacteristically silent while they waited for Cassie to join them, but they did not wait for long. She walked up with her usual smile, but it faded rapidly when she saw their grim expressions. "What's wrong?" she asked, pausing mid-step and looking them all over nervously.

Adam took a deep breath. "My grandma had a massive stroke yesterday. She's in the hospital now, and the doctor says it's not looking good."

Silence hung in the air around the group as they all digested the news. Cassie slid her arms around Adam and hugged him tightly.

"I'm so sorry…"

Adam held her while the rest of his friends patted him on the back. When she let go, he added, "We're also taking in my eight-year-old cousin that my grandma was raising. She can't be left alone, so I'm gonna have to watch her on Saturdays until one of my parents gets home."

Cassie looked like she had been slapped across the face by Adam's revelation. Walter grumbled about knowing what that's like, Ken nodded sagely, Lex stared at the floor as if not knowing what to do or say, and Damien bit his lip. After a moment or two, Damien said, "What if we helped you watch her?"

"What do you mean?" Adam asked with a yawn.

"Yeah! We could look after her so you and Cassie still get to hang out!" Walter chimed in encouragingly.

Adam shrugged. "I mean…she's nervous around strangers, and too much excitement can set her off. She's…not one hundred percent all right in her head."

"Then you can introduce us to her one weekend at a time," Lex suggested.

"It'll help you chill a bit, with your grandma and all," Damien added.

Adam looked at them. Cassie seemed intrigued but had not spoken yet. He had to admit that the idea of not losing his time with Cassie over the weekends was comforting, but he cared too much for his little cousin to think only of himself in the situation.

Then Ken spoke up. "We're your friends. This is what friends do. You'd do the same for one of us."

"Pretty sure you have at one point," Walter added.

Adam chuckled a little then relented. "All right, I'll talk to my mom and see what she thinks of it, then I'll let you guys know tomorrow. Okay?"

"Works for me!" Walter declared cheerfully, with general agreement from the rest of the group.

Cassie offered her hand. "Come on, Adam, it's almost time for class."

Adam took her hand and let her lead him to the classroom. He was far too tired to notice the usual stares and whispered comments. The support of his friends took a little edge off his depression, which left him with just exhaustion. He and Cassie sat down in their usual seats, and no further discussion was made.

For the rest of the day, Cassie treated him with a gentle tenderness Adam was grateful for. His friends all tried their best to lift his spirits at lunch and pledged their support to what Walter had dubbed "Operation: Baby-Sitting."

Three more classes later, Adam was heading back out to the bus for the end of the day, seriously considering taking a nap when he got home. He and Cassie made their usual farewell, then Adam climbed on the bus and looked for Evey. When he found her, he slid into the seat beside her.

Evey immediately asked, "Who was that pretty girl with you?"

"That's Cassie, my girlfriend," Adam replied simply. It still felt strange to call her that aloud.

"She must be special. Your shadow seems to like her."

Adam's drooped eyelids sprang open. The dream from the night before was suddenly vivid in his mind, causing his skin to break out into goosebumps. "Evey, I don't want to be rude, but...could you not talk about my shadow, please?" he asked nervously.

Evey cocked her head with a puzzled look, then shrugged and said, "If you want me not to, I won't. Okay, A. K.?"

"Thanks, Evey," Adam said gratefully.

"Mhm!" she replied cheerfully, humming to herself and kicking her legs as she stared out the window.

When they arrived at home, Evey went to her room, still humming to herself. Adam set his book bag in his room, then went back downstairs to wait for his mom to get home, seating himself in the dining room. An hour later, his mom walked in and greeted him somewhat somberly.

"Hey, nothing to do today?"

"Actually, I wanted to talk to you about something," Adam said, assuming his mother's downcast mood was for the same reason as his own.

"What is it?" she asked, taking her jacket off and hanging it on the dining room chair.

"I know we have to have somebody around Evey at all times. I told my friends today, and Damien was wondering if they might be able to help out."

"Help out how?" she asked, her expression serious.

"One of them could come and watch her for us."

"She'd have to be introduced to them first, and they'd need to know her medications and what not to do around her."

"I figured." His reply was nonchalant enough, but something felt off. His mom seemed agitated.

"If they're willing, I know I'd appreciate it."

"I'll let them know tomorrow," Adam said with a grin.

His mom smiled back weakly and sat down. "I have something to tell you as well."

Adam's brow furrowed slightly. "Yeah?"

His mom took a deep breath. "As of next Monday, I am suspended without pay."

"What?" Adam blurted out, aghast.

She nodded gravely. "I had a minor accident over a month ago. Apparently, the post office higher-ups feel disciplinary action is needed. The union is gonna fight it, but if it takes too long...we could lose the house."

Adam's eyes widened. "Mom..."

"It wasn't even my fault!" Tears filled her eyes.

Adam threw his arms around her, and she sobbed for a few minutes. "We'll figure something out," he assured her.

"I hope so, 'cause we've got nowhere else to go right now," his mom murmured.

"I know, but we'll manage. We always have," Adam insisted. While he was trying to be supportive, he felt his own fear growing upon him. With little Evey now relying on them, losing the house wasn't an option, but what could they do when faced with the unthinkable?

Despite his brave face, Adam was overwhelmed. Things had rapidly gone from good to bad, and then to worse. As he hugged his crying mother, Adam's thoughts were grim. *What else can go wrong?*

12. Distortion

"It burns! It burns!"

Screaming, but no one there to hear. Darkness, then light. Painful light, and the roar of flames engulf his vision.

"Why is this happening?"

Why is what happening? The flames are cold, and so are the bones that feed them. The stench of rot and gore hangs heavy in the air, but with it is a sweet perfume even more stomach-turning than the blood...so much blood...

"There is more," a loathsome hiss snakes its way across his flesh.

The world is awash in green sand, funneling into an empty void. He is falling...falling...

"Stop! Stop it now!" Crash!

The glass explodes with a thousand screaming faces. He sees them all, but none of them are without another. They are one mass of flesh...They're melting, melting into the inky waters.

No, not water.

It's vomit. A sea of black vomit.

Bile burned Adam's throat. He rolled over in bed and sat up, his head splitting with agony. The bombardment of sounds and images left him nauseated. *What the hell was that?* If it was a dream, it had been the most incoherent mess of a dream he'd ever experienced.

Adam pressed his palms to his eyes and tried to recall each image and sound individually, but they flowed seamlessly together. His stomach lurched, and he looked back up at the walls of his bedroom to shake the feeling. Adam stared, trying to let the bizarre dream drift away before finally lying back down and closing his eyes.

Five minutes later, his alarm sounded, and Adam groaned in frustration.

The first order of the day was to wake Evey up and get her moving. Adam blinked grogginess from his eyes and crossed from his bedroom to hers. He gave her door a gentle knock and called, "Evey? Time to get up!"

Evey's voice answered, "I'm already up, A.K.!"

Adam blinked in surprise. "Are you getting ready for school?"

"Yep! Been up for five whole minutes!"

"Oh. Okay." He frowned before heading downstairs for a quick breakfast.

To Adam's surprise, Evey didn't need much of his attention. He was able to go about his morning routine uninterrupted, and sooner than he expected, they were standing at the end of the driveway, waiting for the bus. Evey hummed to herself and swayed back and forth as Adam peered down the dirt road for the bus's headlights. The crickets and other insects chirping from the nearby brush were particularly vocal that morning. *Wonder what's got them all stirred up?* Then, his blood chilled. *No. Not crickets. Voices.*

Adam looked around at the trees, trying to brush the thought away, but there was no denying it. Unintelligible whispers drifted through the bushes and high grass. Adam took a deep, trembling breath and turned his head in every direction, looking for the source, but there was only darkness.

"What are you looking for, A. K?" Evey's voice cut through the noise.

Adam blinked and looked back at her. The whispers were gone, and the drone of insects had returned to its usual level. "I...," he began, unsure of what to say. *You'll only scare her.* "It's nothing, Evey."

Evey cocked her head to the side. "Are you sure? You looked nervous or something."

Adam adjusted his book bag over his shoulder and nodded. "Yeah, it was nothing."

"Ooookay," Evey replied skeptically before the headlights of the school bus finally came into view.

As they climbed on board and took their seats, Adam recalled the whispers. *Was it nothing?* It had to be. There was no one else there besides Evey. Still, as the bus pulled away from the driveway, he scanned the tree line nervously.

"HOLY SHIT," KEN GASPED after Adam related the latest bad news.

The usual banter was absent—no one seemed to know what to say.

"I know," Adam replied miserably. "Seems like we can't catch a break."

"What about the plan for us to meet Evey?" Damien asked.

Adam frowned. "What about it?"

Walter shrugged. "Is it still happening?"

Adam looked to Cassie, who was sitting beside him and holding his hand. Her brilliant eyes were full of concern. He could almost hear her saying she'd understand if they'd have to cancel the plan, but the idea of not being with her was another hit he wasn't prepared to take.

Adam turned back to Damien and Walter and nodded. "We might as well. No telling how long the union will take to sort out this mess." When he finished speaking, Cassie gave his hand a light squeeze.

The mood lightened after that. Adam stayed quiet, basking in Cassie's comforting presence, and his friends returned to their usual raucous selves. Everything seemed almost normal after the upheaval of the past two days. Then the bell rang, and everyone hurried to class without a care. For a moment, Adam was shocked that the world around him still moved as it always had, even though his world was nearly caving in around him. The only one who seemed constantly mindful of his worries was Cassie.

She still met Adam between classes. Though she did nothing more than hold his hand while they walked, Adam was grateful. However, at lunch time, Cassie was nowhere in sight. He waited as long as he dared by his locker, but when she didn't turn up, he made for the cafeteria. *Must've been held up.* Her absence left a knot in his gut, but Adam ignored it, heading for their usual table where Ken and Damien were already seated.

As he sat down, Ken clasped his hands under his chin and propped his elbows on the table. "So, we have some questions."

"'Scuse me?" Adam asked with a frown.

"About the Halloween party," Ken added.

Uh-oh. Adam's eyes widened slightly. "What about it?"

Damien scratched his cheek. "You didn't think we didn't notice when you and Cassie disappeared for about an hour, did you?"

Adam's face suddenly was burning. He took a deep, shaky breath, but before he could speak, Ken raised his hands.

"Don't worry, we don't need details. We're just curious is all."

Adam was mortified. He gulped and stared at his lunchbox. "Well...um...we...went off...and well...we...I guess...We're...I'm not... a virgin...anymore." If Adam had looked into a mirror, he wouldn't have been surprised to see his face melting from its own heat. He glanced up at his friends. Damien was in awe, and Ken had a knowing smile.

Ken said, "I'm happy for you."

"What was it like?" Damien asked eagerly.

Ken frowned at him. "It's enough he told us. Like I said, you don't have to give details."

Thanks, Ken. Adam took another shaky breath, and the burning in his cheeks slowly dissipated. He went about unpacking his lunch.

But Damien's voice grumbled, "I think we're owed details after covering for his ass."

Adam glared at him in shock. "What the hell, man?"

Damien blinked in surprise. "Huh?"

"What do you mean that you're owed details?" Adam accused.

The color drained from Damien's face. "I...I didn't say anything."

"But I just heard you!"

"But I didn't say anything!"

"Adam," Ken interjected, his eyes wide.

"What?" Adam snapped.

"He...He didn't say anything, dude," Ken affirmed with a nervous stare.

"He...He didn't?" The heat of Adam's blush was a distant memory. This time, his skin broke into goosebumps.

"No," Damien replied simply, though he looked almost as scared as Adam felt.

ADAM JOLTED AWAKE THAT night, almost groaning with disappointment. He had been having a thrilling dream about being with Cassie that had left his heart racing. Adam sat for a moment, recalling the familiar velvety touch of her skin and the way it glowed in the moonlight.

Closing his eyes, he lay back down. With any luck, the dream would pick up where it left off. However, the anticipation and his own excitement left sleep out of the question. With a sigh of frustration, Adam went to the bathroom, holding onto the dream as best as he could.

Afterward, as he stepped out of the bathroom, Adam suddenly felt icily cold. Shivering, he climbed back into bed, hoping the covers would chase the sudden chill away. However, even beneath the covers, his teeth chattered. *Did someone leave a window open?*

Adam got up and crept around the house, checking every window he could, but all were closed tightly against the night air that still somehow seemed to have found its way into his very skin. Desperate to shake it, Adam checked the thermostat. His dad liked the house at sixty-eight degrees, and the thermostat's display said nothing was amiss.

Wrapping his arms around himself, Adam crept back up the stairs to his room. On a shelf in his closet was an electric blanket he usually saved for winter. *If that doesn't work, I don't know what will.* He plugged the blanket in, set the dial to the max, spread it across the bed, and crawled under it. Still, despite the blazing heat from the blanket, Adam continued to shiver. *A hot shower. That's gotta do it.* Adam once again headed to the bathroom.

He closed the door and flicked on the light switch. But when the light came on, Adam had to blink to convince himself he wasn't still asleep. He stared at his hand on the switch. A strange shadow shimmered across his skin. Adam held up his other hand, finding that same shadow dancing across it, like a dark reflection off water. His eyes nearly bulged from their sockets, and his throat tightened. The hair on the back of his neck stood on end. Adam stepped in front of the bathroom mirror over the sink.

To his surprise, his perfectly normal reflection looked back at him. Bewildered, he examined his hands again. The shadow was still there. Slowly, Adam peered back up at his reflection, only to find that its eyes had turned entirely black. It then opened its mouth, and Adam heard his own voice say, "You cannot fight forever."

Adam closed his eyes tightly for a moment. *It's not real. It can't be real. It's not there. It's just...a dream.* He then opened his eyes. Once again, his usual reflection was all he saw. To his relief, the shimmering darkness was gone from his hands and the inexplicable cold with it. *Was I sleepwalking?*

As Adam was beginning to take comfort in the idea, the mirror began to rattle.

Adam took a step back, his wide eyes locked on the trembling mirror. Suddenly, his reflection began to change. The flesh around his chin and nose slowly peeled away, revealing a crimson layer of sinew underneath and sharpened teeth. His pale skin darkened to a bluish gray, and tiny horns sprouted from around his forehead, his cheeks, and his chin. As Adam stared into his own eyes, set deep in the face of this hideous monster, they turned completely black.

Adam screamed, and a thundering voice cut through his mind, "Give yourself to me."

Adam jolted awake to the sound of his alarm. He was soaked in sweat and tangled in his bed sheets. His alarm continued its tone, so Adam sat up, unable to tell if what he'd seen had been real or was just an extremely vivid nightmare.

Shaking the chill from his spine, he examined his bed. The heated blanket was nowhere in sight. Nervously, Adam silenced his alarm and climbed out of bed to check the closet. The blanket was still neatly folded in its place on the shelf.

It must have been a dream. Adam repeated the thought to himself and went to wake Evey up. *Just a dream.* All through his morning routine, the thought was echoing in his mind. *Just a dream.*

Still, the things he had seen and felt stuck with him, and throughout the morning, Adam couldn't bring himself to look in a mirror.

"ARE YOU OKAY?" CASSIE asked.

Adam stared at the surface of his desk in Mr. Martinez's room. He and Cassie were seated in their corner alone. "Yeah, why?" he lied.

"You were unusually quiet this morning. Didn't seem like yourself."

"Was it that obvious?"

"I don't know if they noticed, but I did. What's wrong?" Cassie probed.

Adam had wanted to forget the dream, but it lingered in his mind far longer than he'd thought it would. Even there in the brightly lit classroom, it still sent a chill down his spine. "Well...I had a really weird dream last night..." The events of the nightmare replayed in his head, all the way back to when he had thought he'd woken up in the first place. With his recollection came the memory of his dream about Cassie. Suddenly, his face was too hot.

"And?" Cassie asked quietly.

Slowly, Adam turned to look at her. Even after almost two months together, her beauty still took his breath away. The dream of her replayed in his mind, driving the creepiness from it entirely. Adam could think of nothing but Cassie, from the silky feeling of his fingers through her hair to the soft, firmness of her...

Mortified, Adam's eyes darted back up to Cassie's. She raised an eyebrow, but then her lips slowly curled into a sultry smile.

"Is 'weird' really the right word for this dream?"

"N-no," Adam stammered in reply, his cheeks growing redder.

Cassie slid her chair back and leaned forward, propped her elbow on the desk, and rested her chin on her hand. "Tell me about it."

Adam's pulse raced as the dream replayed rapidly in his head. How could he put it into words? His mouth opened and closed several times. Adam thought of how to begin, only to second-guess himself. Cassie waited patiently, her smile never faltering as he floundered with his words.

At last, he began, "W-w-well, we...We were..."

"Good morning!" Mr. Martinez greeted them both as he walked in.

Adam's mouth snapped shut, and he tried to blink away his blush to no avail.

"Good morning, sir!" Cassie answered cheerfully, flipping her hair and leaning back in her seat as though nothing was amiss.

How does she do it? "Morning, sir," Adam replied. As Mr. Martinez set his things on his desk, Adam snuck a glance at Cassie. She flipped her hair and tipped him a wink. He wasn't off the hook yet.

However, Cassie didn't bring the matter up again, even after they left Mr. Martinez's room for their next classes. Adam wrestled with himself all the while, preparing an explanation for her as he sat down in his second-hour room, but his imagination had other ideas. Fantasy after fantasy chased through his mind, each more thrilling than the last. He stared at the empty blackboard while students slowly filled the empty desks around him. His thoughts spun around the velvety feel of Cassie's skin, the sweet taste of her lips, her smoldering crystal-blue eyes, her firm and irresistible...

Adam stopped mid-thought, his breathing accelerating. *If I keep this up, somebody's gonna notice.* He drew in a long, slow breath and focused his attention on the teacher as she entered the room. Once she began speaking,

Adam's fantasies began to fade. He relaxed in his seat, letting the heat coursing throughout his body slowly abate while the lecture continued. *No problem.*

The room lurched.

Adam blinked and shook his head, but the room kept tilting until it seemed to be twisting before his eyes. His stomach heaved. *I'm gonna be sick.* He raised his hand to get the teacher's attention, but then his throat began to burn. *No time.*

Pressing a hand to his mouth, Adam ran for the door. Luckily, the bathroom was just across the hall. He dashed inside, threw his head over the first toilet he came to, and emptied his stomach's contents. His eyes watering, Adam coughed and sputtered, rocked by another heave.

Certain at last that his stomach was settled, Adam slowly sat back on the floor, trembling. *What the hell just happened?* For a moment, he imagined what he had seen once more, but his stomach did a backflip in response, and he thought better of it. *Must've been something I ate.* Not really believing himself, Adam shakily got to his feet and went to the sink to wash his face and hands. The splash of cool water was soothing, abating his quivering until, at last, he looked at himself in the mirror. He certainly had looked better, but at least he wouldn't be sick again.

Then he caught sight of a shadowy figure looming over his shoulder.

Adam yelped in surprise and whirled around, but the bathroom was completely abandoned. He gripped the sink, his heart pounding in his chest.

Get back to class. Now!

Adam dashed out of the bathroom and into the deserted hallway, but the classroom was dark and the door closed.

That can't be right.

He grabbed the door handle and turned, but it was locked.

What the hell?

There was movement in the corner of his vision. Adam glanced down the hallway, and his blood froze. One by one, the overhead fluorescent lights were going out from the end of the hallway, coming toward him. He turned around, but the same was happening at the other end. The darkness beyond the few remaining lights was absolute. Adam pressed his back to the door with nowhere to run, his knuckles white as he gripped the handle uselessly.

At last, only the light directly above him remained. His wide eyes darted from one side of the hall to the other, but the darkness was pitch-black. Shadowy tendrils slithered out of the darkness along the wall across the hall, waving gently in their movements.

Panic welled in Adam's mind, but his muscles would not respond. Slowly, the creeping tendrils pulled themselves off the wall and wrapped themselves around him. He tried to scream, but his mouth remained clamped shut. The shadowy appendages pulled him into the inky blackness beyond the light. Then Adam was falling...falling...falling...

Suddenly, Adam was in the brightly lit cafeteria, surrounded by his friends. He blinked in confusion, glancing at the clock on the wall. It was indeed lunch time. "How...How did I get here?" Adam asked aloud, his eyes bulging from their sockets.

"Uh...the same way you always do?" Damien replied with a frown.

"Yeah, you came in and sat down just like normal, man," Walter confirmed.

"I...I don't remember...," Adam began, his breathing spiraling out of control. Where had he been for the last two hours? Why was it all blank?

Cassie placed a calming hand on his shoulder. "You're going through a lot right now. It only makes sense you'd be too distracted to remember your everyday routine. You probably went on autopilot."

"Yeah, you were pretty quiet all this morning," Ken added.

"I..." But then Adam closed his mouth and stared at the table. Was that all it was? Was the stress getting to him more than he realized, or was he losing his grip completely?

He let Cassie's presence calm his mind, but he still couldn't shake the fear of what had happened in that missing two hours.

"LET THEM ROT!"

But they're not rotting. They're growing. The angry voices are growing. Getting louder.

"Kill us all!"

Why do they want to die? Why would anyone want to die? The floor of the afterlife is covered with hands, grasping at him as he falls, tearing him apart...

Booooooom!

His head might split open from the thunderous blast. It pierces his chest like ice but colder. He's growing colder. He's losing himself. He's losing everything...

Adam snapped out of the sensory bombardment, finding himself standing in Evey's room. It was dark, but Evey's light was on, and she was sitting up on her bed, looking at him expectantly.

Oh no, not again. "E...Evey?" Adam asked shakily.

Evey frowned. "What, A.K.?"

"H-h-how...How did I g-g-g-get here?"

Evey giggled in response. "Through the door, dummy!"

Panic was once again building in Adam's chest. He remembered going to bed, but as far as he knew, he had never gotten up. Adam struggled to control his breathing and backed toward the door.

"Aren't you gonna tell me what I'm supposed to do?" she asked.

Adam looked at her, fighting with all his might to keep the terror out of his eyes. "Excuse me?"

"You said you needed me to do something!"

"Ummm...no, I didn't."

"Yes, you did!" Evey squeaked.

Adam held a finger to his lips. "Shhhhhh!"

"Oh! Shhhhhhh." Evey copied him, pressing her own finger to her lips with a mischievous grin. She was playing with him, but Adam was far from in the mood.

He sat on her bed and mumbled, "What was I talking about?"

Evey whispered her reply, "You said you had to do something, and that I'd have to do something, too, to help you. Don't you remember?"

Adam wracked his brain, but none of it sounded familiar. "I...I must have been sleepwalking." His thoughts revisited the bizarre dreams for a moment. Maybe that had something to do with it? Maybe Cassie was right.

None of this makes any sense.

13. Escape

The following morning, Adam entered the cafeteria doors as usual. However, the moment he crossed the threshold, his ears were bombarded with a cacophony of voices. Blinking repeatedly in bewilderment, Adam looked around the cafeteria. There couldn't have been more than a dozen students there at the time, and while they did appear to be conversing casually, the voices he was hearing had to be at least double their number.

Adam traced his usual steps to his locker, then to the couches in the front entryway, but the voices didn't go away. In fact, when his friends arrived, things only got worse. People passed by through the hallways, and a few more groups gathered on the neighboring couches. The voices grew louder. Try as he might, Adam couldn't hide the agony of it. His face tightened, and he stared at the ceiling, his head splitting from the noise.

"Are you okay?" Lex's voice cut through, but the drone continued unabated.

Adam closed his eyes and answered through gritted teeth, "Just...Just a nasty headache." *God, make it stop!*

Walter suggested, "Maybe you should go to class early. It'll be quieter."

"Hey, guys!" Cassie's voice piped up, and suddenly, the noise vanished.

Adam opened his eyes, unable to hide the shock in them. The noise level was back to normal, and if Adam didn't know better, he'd think Cassie had something to do with it. He heaved a sigh of relief and got up. "That's not a bad idea."

"What's not?" Cassie asked, but Adam grabbed her hand, and together, they headed off to class. Once they were seated, Adam reveled in the silence, the drone of that morning now completely gone.

Cassie cocked her head at him. "Are you okay?"

Adam heaved another sigh and said, "I'm better now that you're here."

Cassie flushed a little and flipped her hair to flash him a warm smile. "That's sweet of you." Adam's cheeks reddened, but then she asked, "So are we going to be able to get together this weekend?"

"If Ken can give me a ride," Adam answered.

"Why don't you ask him at lunch?"

"I think I will," Adam agreed as Mr. Martinez walked in with his usual cheerful greeting.

TO ADAM'S SURPRISE, nothing amiss happened for the rest of the day. Ken agreed readily enough to be his chauffeur for the weekend, and the weirdness of the morning was all but forgotten by the last class. Everything seemed to be getting back to normal.

Then Adam noticed the classroom had grown deathly silent. He frowned and glanced around at the other students, but what he saw froze the blood in his veins. There were just under twenty students in the classroom, and every single one of them was staring at him. Their faces wore the same vacant expression, and their eyes were wide and unblinking. As Adam opened his mouth to ask what was going on, each student's eyes rolled back, and their mouths distended, emitting an ear-splitting shriek.

With a scream of horror, Adam leapt from his desk and ran for the door, the screeching ringing in his ears even as he dashed out into the hallway. A janitor was outside with his mop and bucket, but the moment he turned to look at Adam, his eyes rolled back, and he emitted the same piercing wail. Panicked, Adam ran for the main entrance, passing a pair of conversing teachers and a student council member. Each reacted to him the same way as the students in class and the janitor. Overwhelmed with terror, Adam threw himself onto one of the couches and buried his face in his trembling hands.

Moments later, he heard the voice of Miss Umber, the school nurse, beside him. "Adam? Are you okay?"

"I...I don't know," he replied shakily, unwilling to raise his face from his hands to look at her.

"Can you look at me, please?"

"No!" Adam exclaimed, turning his face away from her.

Miss Umber was silent for a moment before saying softly, her voice full of both concern and alarm, "Just...let me get the counselor real quick."

Adam did not reply as she hurried away. What was happening to him? Why was he seeing these things? Was the stress making him crack, or were the weird dreams depriving him of real sleep, making him hallucinate? He didn't feel extremely tired, but what else could it be? None of this made any sense.

The counselor, Mrs. Fossler, arrived seconds later. "Adam, what's going on? Miss Umber said you refused to look at her."

"I...I think...I think I need to go home," he answered. How could he tell her what he was seeing? What would she think of it? *He* didn't know what to think of it.

"Let me call your parents, and I'll see what I can do. In the meantime, Miss Umber is gonna stay here with you, all right?" When Adam nodded in reply, Mrs. Fossler left.

Miss Umber said nothing as they both waited, Adam still keeping his eyes away from her. If he saw another face morph into a screaming *thing*, he might have a panic attack.

Adam had no way of knowing how much time had passed, but soon, the office door opened, and Mrs. Fossler called, "I've spoken with your mother, Adam. She's waiting for you out front. You may go with her."

"Th-thank you," Adam called, slowly getting up and heading for the front doors, keeping his eyes fixed to the floor all the while.

After Adam got into his mom's car and they were pulling away, she asked, "Can you tell me what happened?"

Adam stared at the dashboard, unwilling to make eye contact. "I...I think I had...some kind of breakdown. I just..." He shuddered, recalling the distending mouths and rolling eyes. Worst of all was the ear-splitting shrieking that had come with it. Gulping, Adam said, "I...I think it was some kind of panic attack or something..."

His mom didn't say anything for a moment, but then she burst into tears. "This is all my fault!"

Adam blinked and turned to look at her, his fear completely forgotten. "No, it's not!"

"Yes, it is!" she sobbed. "Too much is happening, and you...you shouldn't be dealing with all this...but..."

"Mom, it's okay." Adam tried to reassure her by placing a hand on her shoulder. "We're all going through a lot. It's nobody's fault, all right? It's just...It's a lot."

His mom sighed and wiped her eyes. "Still...I feel..."

"Forget it," Adam insisted. "Don't blame yourself. I just...I guess I'm a bit overwhelmed. That's all."

His mom took a deep breath. "You know...you're right. Maybe you need a quiet day to process everything. The night we brought Evey over, everything just kind of happened so fast, and then you were back in school and all...Maybe you just need a day off to collect yourself."

Adam bit his lip. A day at home certainly sounded appealing, but he didn't like the idea of losing any time with Cassie. Deciding to be honest, he said, "I would like that, but...I want to see Cassie too..."

As they pulled into their driveway, his mom added, "Why don't you have her come over after school, then?"

Adam smiled. "That would work just fine!"

"As long as you guys don't go upstairs alone together," she warned.

"Not a problem. I'll talk to her about it tonight on the phone." A full day off from school *and* spending the evening with Cassie? Maybe things were looking up after all.

THAT NIGHT, SOMETHING hitting his window woke Adam. He blinked and sat up, frowning. *What had that been? A bird, or a bat?* He stared at the window for a moment, considering lying back down, but something hit it again with a sharp thud.

What the hell? Adam slid out of bed, pulled up the blinds, and took a look outside. To his surprise, Cassie was standing in the backyard in her long coat. She waved to him and smiled, dropping a pair of rocks by her side. Adam held up a finger and mouthed *wait* before doubling back into his room. He grabbed a woolen robe and threw it on over his pajamas before creeping down the stairs and out the side door. Adam found Cassie waiting for him exactly where she had been when he saw her from the window.

"How'd you get here?" he whispered.

Cassie grinned. "I took a walk." She stepped up to him. "I figured you needed me after what happened this afternoon."

Adam smiled gratefully. "I suppose it can't hurt." They had discussed everything over the phone earlier that evening, but nothing compared to seeing her in person. "You're still coming over tomorrow, though, right?"

"Of course," Cassie assured him with a smile, "but tomorrow, I won't be able to do this." She then grabbed him by the front of his robes and kissed him voraciously.

Adam wasn't sure if he remembered to breathe or not. By the time Cassie pulled away from him, he was lightheaded, but he smiled, nonetheless. "I'm glad you came."

Cassie flipped her hair and tilted her head, fluttering her eyelashes as she smiled at him. "So, what do you want to do? Tonight's about making you feel better."

Adam thought a moment. He'd love for them to cuddle in his bed, but it would be insanely risky. There was always the barn, however. Adam nodded toward it. "Why don't we go in there?"

Cassie nodded. "All right, lead the way."

Adam took her hand and led her into the barn. There was no light inside, so Cassie turned on the flashlight on her phone. The costumes had been cleaned up and put away, leaving the interior as empty as ever.

Adam took off his robe and spread it out on the ground for them to lay on. They snuggled together as the lit-up phone sat nearby.

Cassie whispered in his ear, "Are you happy like this?"

Adam smiled at her. "Could hardly be happier."

Cassie stroked his cheek with her free hand. "Wanna bet?"

SHE LEFT A FEW HOURS later, and Adam crept back to his bed in a state of euphoria. He fell asleep easily and woke up still riding the high after his mom had taken Evey to school and his dad had left for work. Adam spent the day going back and forth between reading and video games, enjoying the quiet time to himself.

Then, almost a half-hour after Evey got home, Cassie was at the front door in her usual baggy clothes. Adam let her in, and she greeted him with a hug and a kiss on the cheek. "How are you feeling?"

"Pretty good," Adam answered with a grin, pulling away to close the door behind her.

"A. K.! I wanna meet your girlfriend!" Evey called from upstairs.

"All right, Evey, come on down!" His mom must have told her that Cassie was coming over.

Evey hurried down the stairs but stopped dead as soon as she saw Cassie. "Oh...Aunt Patty wasn't kidding. You're even prettier up close!"

Cassie grinned wide and pressed her hands to her cheeks excitedly. "I had no idea your cousin was so adorable!"

Evey ran up to her to take her hand, but then she stopped and looked at Adam. "Can I take her upstairs to see my room?"

Adam shrugged. "I don't see why not."

"Come on!" Evey cried excitedly, leading a beaming Cassie up the stairs.

"Let me know if you need anything!" Adam sat in the living room, all the while listening to Evey exclaiming about her drawings and Cassie gushing in turn. Their exchanges made Adam smile.

The rest of the evening passed uneventfully. Cassie ate dinner with Adam and his family, and they watched a movie together in the living room. When it was time for her to leave, Adam walked her down to the end of the driveway.

As she stepped out onto the road, she turned to him and said, "I can take it from here. I had a great time today."

"You're gonna walk?" Adam gasped.

Cassie shrugged. "I like walking. Anyways...will I see you at school tomorrow?"

"I should be there."

"Good." Cassie fluttered her eyelashes, but then her arms were around him, and their lips were pressed together.

He couldn't tell how long it lasted, but when Cassie left, she waved to him seductively before heading down the road.

Adam watched her go, unable to stop the grin spreading across his features. Maybe things were going to be all right after all.

THAT NIGHT, ADAM HAD yet another sensory-overloading nightmare. He knew he was dreaming, but the bombardment of his senses was unyielding.

Wake up!

Adam tried to urge himself out of the hellish kaleidoscope of horror and death, but the harder he fought, the faster the sounds and images flew by, until he couldn't make out any details at all. Surely, the sheer force of imagery was going to tear his head wide open.

God, make it stop!

With a cry of terror, Adam snapped out of it. However, he wasn't in his bed. He was once again standing in Evey's room in the middle of the night. A lamp on a dresser beside her bed was lit up.

Adam grabbed the edge of the dresser to steady himself, still dizzy from the barrage of images, but then he heard harsh breathing and grunts of frustration coming from Evey's bed. He looked up. Evey was sitting up, her eyes wide as she scratched furiously at her wrist.

Shit! Adam looked frantically for Evey's drawing materials, but they were nowhere in sight. Without knowing where they were, he had no choice but to try and stop her from tearing her wrist open to draw with her own blood. Adam leapt onto the bed and pinned her down. She screamed and thrashed against him with more force than her eight-year-old body should have been capable of.

Seconds later, both his mom and dad came running in. "What the hell is going on!" his dad demanded.

"Find her drawing stuff!" Adam cried, wrestling to keep Evey's arms pinned down. She snarled in anger and snapped at Adam with her teeth, but his arms were long enough to keep out of her reach.

Seconds later, piles of papers and colored pencils were thrown onto the bed. As quickly as he could manage, Adam released Evey and jumped back. She rolled over and snatched up one of the colored pencils before drawing furiously on one of the sheets of paper. Evey tore through but didn't seem to notice, just kept drawing.

Adam tried to catch his breath, astounded by Evey's strength. He had heard about how scary one of her episodes could be, but witnessing it firsthand was something else entirely. "Where were they?" he asked his parents as he regained himself.

"Tucked neatly in one of the dresser drawers," his dad replied without looking away from Evey.

"I wonder what set her off," his mother whispered.

Adam bit his lip as the barest sliver of his nightmare danced through his mind. "Me too."

Adam stayed with Evey for almost an hour until her drawing slowed and her pictures began to take on more coherent shapes. Her eyes shifted back into focus, and Adam was certain she had finally come out of her episode. "Evey?" he whispered gently.

Evey glanced up at him. "Oh, hi, A. K.!"

"What happened to your drawing things last night? We found them tucked away in a drawer when you wanted them."

Evey bit her lip before answering, "I wanted Cassie to come back. If I cleaned my room, I'd get to see her again, right?"

Adam let out a breath, releasing the tightness in his chest. "You don't need to put your things away for her to come back. She likes coming around."

"She does?" Evey tittered excitedly.

Adam nodded and yawned. "Yep. Now, come on. We need to get ready for school."

14. Conflict

Cassie's alarm beeped obnoxiously. With a groan, she stirred awake, trying to hold onto the fragments of a very pleasant dream about Adam. However, as she came to, she realized she was also holding onto her bunched-up blanket as though it *were* Adam. Blushing, Cassie pushed the blankets away and rolled out of bed. *It can't be healthy to be* that *needy.* As she went about getting ready for school, she reminded herself that every time they were together could be their last. Perhaps it was all right to want to be around him so much in that case.

At school, Cassie headed for the couches in the entryway, eager to see Adam again. His staying home had made the day a chore, but the time spent with him before and after more than made up for it. She was looking forward to having him with her before and between classes again.

However, when she arrived, Adam was nowhere in sight. His friends were all gathered as usual, but Adam was absent. Cassie's smile faded when Walter and Damien turned suspicious eyes in her direction. Ken looked uncharacteristically uncomfortable, and Lex was watching Walter and Damien with an air of unease that made Cassie nervous. "Umm...where's Adam?" she asked, unable to hide her mounting anxiety.

Damien huffed. "Apparently, he didn't want to hang out with us this morning."

Oh no. Cassie's heart clenched. "Why not? What's wrong?"

Walter was about to speak, but Lex heaved a sigh. "It's nothing, really."

Certainly doesn't seem like nothing. Cassie backed away slowly. "I...I'll go talk to him." She turned and started off in the direction of their first class.

"Hey, Cassie, wait up!" came Ken's voice after she made it halfway down the hall. She stopped and turned around, and Ken walked up to her. "Look, Adam's been acting really strange all week, and it seems like the only person he wants to be around lately is you."

Cassie's eyes narrowed. "Is that really *my* fault?"

Ken held up his hands disarmingly. "Hey, Lex and I get it. He's going through hell right now, and you fill a void for him that me and the guys can't. I get it...but Walt and Damien don't."

Cassie rolled her eyes. "They could afford to be a little more understanding, then."

"You should also be understanding of them too," Ken countered, though he kept his voice soft. "We've all been friends for a very long time. When one of us is threatened, we close ranks, but this situation with Adam is like he's pushing us away. It's not like him."

Not like him. They're saying he's not himself. Cassie blanched. "I...I gotta talk to him." She backed away from Ken, unable to keep her fear hidden. *Has Asmodeous taken over already?*

On the edge of panic, Cassie dashed off to the classroom.

Adam was sitting in their usual spot, staring blankly at his computer desk. Dark circles were beginning to form around his eyes, and he looked a little paler than usual.

"A-Adam?" she asked as she approached.

Adam looked at her, and his face lit up immediately. "Hey, Cass!"

Cassie smiled back with relief...despite a strange hollow feeling in her chest she couldn't quite explain. Was it disappointment? *Just who am I hoping to see when I look at him anyways?* As Cassie sat down beside Adam, she wasn't sure of the answer.

Their first class passed as normal. Cassie walked with Adam to his second class, as she had dozens of times, before setting off for her own class. On the way, she almost bumped into Taylor, who was heading for the same class.

"Hey! You okay?"

Cassie blinked and looked at her, unable to hide the worry in her eyes. "I'm fine. I guess I was just distracted."

Taylor's brow furrowed with concern. "You're worried about Adam."

Cassie bit her lip and nodded. Taylor gave her a consoling hug. Cassie closed her eyes for a moment, savoring the embrace before Taylor released her.

"I heard about what happened Tuesday. Is he okay? It's really not like him to freak out like that. Some people thought he got suspended over it or something."

Cassie shook her head. "Nothing like that. He's just going through a lot right now, and I don't think he's sleeping well either. His mom let him stay home for the day to recoup a bit."

Taylor smiled. "That's really cool of her. Good thing he's got two awesome women looking out for him."

Despite herself, Cassie smiled, and her cheeks warmed slightly. As the pair of them headed off to their class together, she found herself wishing she'd made friends with Taylor sooner.

THE SCHOOL DAY WENT on as it normally did until the whole gang was gathered at lunch. Though his friends carried on with their usual antics, Adam was strangely withdrawn. Despite herself, Cassie kept a wary eye on him, though she was still unable to decide if it was out of fear or anticipation.

"Come on, man! It's all about the beards!" said Damien.

"Elves are better archers!" Walter fired back.

"Dwarfs are better engineers," countered Damien, looking smug.

Cassie almost rolled her eyes. *They're arguing about fantasy races.*

"Yeah, but are dwarfs immortal?"

"Are elves?"

"They live long enough!"

"So do dwarfs!"

Walter turned to Adam. "Hey, we need an expert opinion. Which is better: elves or dwarfs?"

"Neither," Adam replied coldly.

Walter blinked in confusion. "Huh?"

Adam explained, "In terms of battlefield effectiveness, there is no more efficient force than one comprised of the undead. They require neither food nor drink, they never need to sleep, and often, the fallen of both friend and foe can rise to swell their ranks. As long-lived as dwarfs or elves are, they are still mortal, and the undead could starve them both into surrender. Think about it—the undead have no need of supply chains or even proper camps. They can attack all day and night, and they never become fatigued. It's a war of attrition that no living thing can hope to win."

The table was silent following Adam's monologue. Cassie was in awe. It had been Adam's voice, but it almost sounded like the kind of things Asmodeous would say. If there was one thing Cassie had learned about Asmodeous over thirteen years, it was that he had a sharp mind for strategy and tactics.

She couldn't help but smile, but then she caught sight of the rest of the guys from the corner of her eye. Walter's mouth hung open in disbelief, Damien's brow was furrowed, Lex's eyes were wide, and Ken was looking at Adam as though he'd just confessed to murder. *Was it really that odd?*

THAT NIGHT, CASSIE would not have as pleasant a dream as she had woken up from in the morning. As she drifted off, she heard Asmodeous's voice whisper from the surrounding darkness, "Cassandra...you have failed me..."

"No!" Cassie cried. "I did everything you asked!"

However, Asmodeous spoke no more. Suddenly, Cassie was back in the woods, surrounded by the five jocks. She tried to slip between them and escape, but they grabbed her and started pushing her around in the circle.

"Stop! Let me go!" she pleaded, but they only laughed.

Ian said, "Time to see what you're hiding under all those baggy clothes!"

"No!" Cassie screamed, but they closed the circle tighter and continued pushing her around, ripping off pieces of her clothing as she bounced from one to the other. She sobbed uncontrollably and tried to cover herself until she was finally stripped naked. The boys laughed raucously, and Cassie sank to the ground in a fetal position, her tears flowing freely. She closed her eyes and covered her ears until she couldn't hear the laughs anymore.

Then there was silence.

Cassie opened her eyes again, but the jocks were gone. She sat up and looked around, only to find the body of her sister, Ally, lying beside her. Her black hair was splayed out and soaked with blood, just as it had been when Cassie had found her before, and her blue eyes were glazed over.

To Cassie's horror, a far too familiar face stood over her. It was a tall, thin man with swept-back black hair and a cruel sneer, dressed in a bloodied white shirt with black pants and suspenders. *Sam.*

Sam laughed cruelly, wiping a bloody kitchen knife on his shirt before pointing at Cassie. He hissed, "You're next, little girl!"

Cassie made to back away, but then a hand clamped down on her shoulder from behind. Kaleb's loathsome voice whispered in her ear, "But only after I've had my way with you."

She jolted awake, gasping for breath and trembling violently. Cassie buried her face in her knees and rocked back and forth, wrestling with the terror threatening to overwhelm her. The urge to scream was almost too much to resist, but that would only bring Darcy—or worse—to her door, and no one in the house could offer her comfort.

Cassie sobbed as quietly as she could manage, desperate to release the panic the dream had brought on. Slowly, her shaking eased, and her rocking slowed.

Cassie's fear ebbed away, and a numbness settled into her limbs, like she had run several miles. She was dizzy from breathing so hard, but that was slowly easing as she fought for control. Cassie gingerly stretched out her legs—they ached with the tension of her panic attack—and lay back down on the bed.

Exhaustion crept up on her slowly, but she couldn't ignore what the dream had told her. She missed the safety Asmodeous's presence promised. If not for him, Sam would have killed her, Kaleb would have molested her, or the jocks would have gang-raped her.

With a miserable sigh, Cassie tried to relax her mind to get some rest, but the dream had stripped away any illusion of comfort. Until Asmodeous took control, she was on her own.

THE FOLLOWING MORNING, Cassie hurried to the couches. Despite her best efforts, she was still shaken by the dream from the night before and all the terrible thoughts that came with it. When she arrived, the whole gang, Adam included, were gathered, but they seemed embroiled in serious conversation.

"I'm sorry, guys," Adam was saying. "This week has just been a crapshoot from start to finish. I didn't mean to take it out on you guys."

Cassie felt a surge of affection for Adam in his sincerity. *He's so sweet.* However, she wondered if any of this would matter once Asmodeous took over. Was Adam wasting his effort trying to mend his relationship with his friends?

Would Asmodeous try to maintain it or just abandon it altogether? Was this only going to make things worse if he did?

Cassie's eyes began to threaten tears. Unwilling to cry in front of anyone except Adam, she turned and headed for her usual spot in the English classroom. None of the guys had seemed to notice her...or so she thought.

Adam came in soon after, looking worried. "Cassie? Are you all right?"

"I...I..." She fumbled her words, a million emotions racing through her exhausted mind. Who did she need more, Adam or Asmodeous? Who was better for her? Who cared more about her? Despite the cacophony in her brain, Cassie replied, "I...I didn't want to interrupt. It's just..." How could she even begin to explain anything?

Adam sat down beside her, his face full of concern.

Finally, she admitted, "I just...had a really, really, *really* bad dream last night, and I didn't...I didn't want to lose it in front of the guys."

"Cassie...," Adam whispered softly, pulling her into his embrace, and she fell into his arms, reveling in their comforting warmth. "Do you want to talk about the dream?"

"No!" Cassie exclaimed quickly, pulling away. But then she smiled apologetically. "I...I'm sorry. I just...What I need is...I just...I don't want to be alone right now."

Adam hugged her again, and Cassie melted in his arms. "We'll have all day together tomorrow, at least."

Cassie nodded without looking at him. *If you only knew...*

Adam then tilted her chin up so they were eye to eye. "Remember how Wednesday night was all about making me feel better?"

Cassie nodded with a small smile.

"Well, tomorrow will be your turn. I promise."

As Adam hugged her once more, Cassie smiled and said with the deepest sincerity, "I can't wait."

THE NEXT DAY FOUND Cassie and Adam back in their grove together. Cassie lay beneath a blanket with her head on his chest, tracing patterns, just as she had the night of the Halloween party. She was completely spent. Without knowing if each time would be their last, she had been desperate to make love to him again and again. Each time only got better, which only fueled her desire for him. It was a cycle Cassie wasn't sure she wanted to end.

Though she didn't want to admit it, Cassie could tell that Adam was slipping away slowly. However, whenever he was with Cassie, he seemed just like the sweet boy she had fallen in love with. Still, as she lay beside him, she couldn't help but miss Asmodeous. She hadn't seen any sign of him since Halloween night, other than Adam's bizarre lunchtime monologue. Asmodeous had practically raised her, been with her every second since she was three years old, and to not have him around was agonizingly lonely.

Cassie's heart began to ache. The more she thought about it, the more it seemed like choosing one would mean losing the other. A part of her wanted Adam to stay Adam and for them to be together forever, but another part wanted Asmodeous back. *It's not fair.* Asmodeous was the closest thing she had to a father, but every day only made her fall more in love with Adam. How could she choose?

Tears filled Cassie's eyes. Her internal argument was tearing her apart. Asmodeous protected her, but Adam made her feel special and appreciated. Adam was observant and insightful, but nothing compared to Asmodeous's wisdom. His advice had never steered her wrong, but she never felt more alive than when she was with Adam. He made her forget to hate how beautiful she was and to even appreciate it for the way it made him look at her.

Cassie sat up, the pain building inside her becoming too much to bear. Adam looked at her, his dark eyes full of concern.

"What's wrong?"

Cassie bit her lip and rubbed her shoulder nervously. *I could tell him. I should* tell him. *He deserves to know. He deserves better...than me. God, what have I done to him? But...if I tell him, he'll leave me. I...I...* Cassie's thoughts trailed off, and her tears flowed freely. "It's nothing," she choked, but it was the least believable lie she had ever told.

Adam placed a hand on her back. "You know you can tell me anything. You know that, right?"

No, I can't. The pain was unbearable. Cassie grabbed her clothes from the pile nearby and slowly got dressed. "I...I think I need to go."

"Go? Did...Did I do something wrong...?"

No. You've done nothing wrong. All of this would be so much easier if you had. All of this would be so much easier if you weren't so fucking perfect. Cassie couldn't hold back anymore. She sobbed. "It...It's not you. It's me. I just...need a minute...alone." But being alone was the very last thing she wanted. She wanted nothing more than to dive back into Adam's arms and drown herself in him. Cassie had never wanted anything more in her life...and never felt less like she deserved it. Once she was fully dressed, she left Adam in silence.

Why did it have to turn out like this? Obeying Asmodeous's every request had never been a problem before. He had done more for her than she could have ever done for him, but her role in putting Asmodeous into Adam was tearing her apart from the inside out. He had been nothing but the sweetest boy she had ever known from the moment they met. Pretending to like him had come easily enough, until Cassie realized she wasn't pretending. By then, "like" had turned to "love," and she couldn't bear the thought of losing him. In time, Asmodeous would surely take control, and Adam, the love of her life, would be gone...

"Cassie?"

Cassie snapped out of her thoughts and turned to see a tall, dark-haired man on the sidewalk in front of her house. She had almost walked right past him, lost in her own internal debate. Now, however, her trepidation evaporated, and in its place was fear. "Do I know you?"

"No," the stranger stated simply. He wore a simple, blue hooded sweatshirt over black jeans and matching tennis shoes. The man was moderately muscular, at least a few years older than Cassie, with a clean-shaven face, brown eyes, and short dark-brown hair. "We never met, but I knew your sister."

Cassie suddenly felt as though she couldn't breathe. "I...I don't have a sister," she lied.

"You did once. She was quite dear to me. Her name was Ally Corbant."

Cassie's eyes widened. She opened her mouth to speak, but no words came. Her throat suddenly felt far too small. After several attempts, she managed to stammer, "H-how..."

The stranger held up his hands disarmingly. "Don't worry, I'm not gonna hurt you. I just want to know what happened that night...the night Ally died."

The memories surged through Cassie's mind with alarming sharpness. Her chest tightened, and she suddenly felt far too exposed on the sidewalk. She backed away, shaking her head and saying, "No...I...I don't want to...to talk about it. Go away."

The man bit his lip before replying, "No one knows what happened that night. People talk, but it's all just hearsay. You're the only one who was there; otherwise, I wouldn't trouble you. I need to know what happened."

"Leave me alone!" Cassie shrieked, turning and running back across the street toward the woods.

"Cassie, come back!" the stranger called, but she didn't look back.

She wanted the safety of her grove. Cassie didn't even turn aside as a car honked and screeched to a halt before nearly running into her. The stranger called again, but all that was on Cassie's mind was escape. She bolted through the woods, hoping against hope that Adam was still at the grove.

15. Terrible Truths

Adam sat bewildered for a moment before dressing himself. He wanted to go after Cassie, but she had said she needed a minute alone. Should he wait for her to come back, or should he just head home? She had seemed pretty upset, so who knew how long she would be? Besides, the sun was inching toward dusk. Even if she came back, they most likely wouldn't have much more time together as it was. Reluctantly, Adam pulled his phone out and texted Ken to come get him.

Adam waited in silence, his mind wracked with worry. What had come over Cassie so suddenly? They had spent an amazing several hours in the grove together, and she had seemed happy, but when all was done and they were just lying together, she suddenly had a complete breakdown. Adam hated to question someone he cared so much about, but it was clear there was something she wasn't telling him, and it was eating away at her. What could it be?

Adam brushed a few chips of bark and dirt from his clothes before turning in the direction of the parking lot. As he was leaving, however, someone came crashing through the trees behind him. He turned around to find Cassie running toward him. Before he could react, she threw her arms around him and started sobbing.

"Cassie...I...." Adam began.

"Adam...there's...this man...He...," Cassie gasped between sobs.

Adam froze; that was not what he had expected to hear. "What happened?" he asked in earnest.

"In front of my house...this man...He stopped me...asked things...I got scared...I'm so glad you're still here..."

"What did he...?"

Adam heard an unfamiliar voice call for Cassie.

"Oh God, it's him!" she whimpered.

Adam's phone vibrated in his pocket; Ken had arrived. "Ken's here. Come on!" Without question, Cassie took his hand, and they fled through the woods.

With the noise they were making, Adam couldn't tell if they were being pursued or not.

Without looking back, the pair raced through the trees and across the street to the cafeteria parking lot where Ken waited. Adam threw open the back door, and he and Cassie slid in.

"Get us outta here!" Adam demanded.

"What the hell...?" Ken started to ask.

Cassie shouted, "Floor it!"

Cassie's panicked voice must have said enough to Ken. He threw the car into drive and headed out of the parking lot. As he turned onto the street, the man that must have been Cassie's pursuer walked out into the middle of the road, waving his arms as if to flag them down.

"Who the fuck is that?" Ken asked.

"Hit him!" Cassie sobbed.

Ken's eyes went wide with disbelief. "What...?"

"HIT HIM!" Cassie shrieked.

The stranger made no move to get out of their way. Ken accelerated, probably hoping to scare him. Seconds later, Adam's stomach clenched—they were about to run the man over. At the last moment, the man leapt aside, and Ken swerved the opposite direction. The car fishtailed before Ken regained control. Adam looked out the back window to see if the stranger was following them. Thankfully, he was not.

Cassie clung to Adam, sobbing hysterically.

Ken looked at them in the rearview mirror. "Can I get an explanation now?" he demanded.

"Cassie went home for a bit," Adam explained, "but apparently, this guy was lurking out front. He stopped her and she got scared, so she came back. He came after her, so we ran. The rest you already know."

Ken didn't say anything, but Adam could tell he was weirded out. "What did this guy want?"

Cassie gave a violent shudder and buried her face in Adam's chest, sobbing afresh.

Adam had never imagined something could rattle her so thoroughly. He looked at Ken and stroked her hair comfortingly. "Best not to ask right now."

Cassie glanced up at Adam, tears staining her cheeks. "Can we...go somewhere...?"

"I can take you to my place. Mom's out on errands, and once she's done, she's going to work for the night," Ken offered.

Cassie looked at Adam with fearful eyes and begged, "Don't make me sleep alone tonight...please."

"What are you gonna tell your parents?" Adam didn't want to leave her alone either, but he doubted they'd let her stay with two boys.

Cassie thought for a moment. "I...I'll tell them that Taylor invited me over for the night."

"Think she'll vouch for you if they ask?" Ken interjected.

Cassie nodded. "I'll text her so she knows."

"All right," Adam said. "Looks like we're crashing with you tonight."

"There's a spare bedroom you can hole up in. Won't be a problem," Ken assured them.

A few minutes later, Ken pulled into the driveway at his house. The drive led up to a small garage next to an only slightly larger backyard. A privacy fence outlined the boundaries of the yard, except where it met the house and the driveway. Ken parked the car, and the three of them got out. He led the way across the deck to the back door, which led into a tiny kitchen. While Ken hung his car keys on a key rack next to the door, Adam led Cassie through a small dining room to the black sofa in the living room. They sat down as Ken entered the room.

"I don't mean to be rude, but I need to know a few things."

Cassie was still attached to Adam's side, but she looked at him and nodded. Adam bristled protectively, but he reminded himself that this was one of his best friends.

"We'll do our best."

Ken sat in a nearby recliner that matched the sofa. He turned to face them both. "So, who was that guy?"

Cassie mumbled, "Not a clue."

"I've never seen him before either," Adam added.

Ken frowned. "Neither have I. What did he want with you?"

Cassie shuddered again but didn't answer.

Adam's stomach turned over. For a moment, he felt a surge of anger toward the stranger. "Probably what most guys want from her."

Ken narrowed his eyes. "Sounds like you might have a stalker." When Cassie said nothing, he asked, "Why didn't you go home?"

Cassie looked at the floor before answering. "I...I guess I panicked."

Ken raised an eyebrow but said nothing. He was obviously suspicious. Truth be told, Adam was too. Still, his first priority was making sure Cassie was okay.

"I watched as we drove away," Adam said. "I'm pretty sure the guy didn't get a good look at your license plate. We're clear on the other side of town. There's no way he could've followed us." Ken didn't seem convinced, so Adam continued, "We'll just stay here tonight and get things figured out tomorrow."

The air was tense for a moment, and Adam wondered if Ken might kick them out, but in the end, he said, "Okay. You're not the first refugees I've taken in anyways."

Both Adam and Cassie sighed with relief.

"Thank you." Adam started digging out his phone. "I better let Mom know right away." He went to her number in his contacts and hit the call button.

She picked up after only two rings. "Hello?"

"Hey, Mom. Is it okay if I stay the night at Ken's?" Adam wondered if she would say no. It wouldn't take much for her to guess that Cassie might stay over as well.

However, to his surprise, she said, "That's fine."

Adam was glad she couldn't see him then. The relief on his face would have been impossible to hide. "How did Lex and Evey get along?"

"Great, actually. Lex might have a knack for this sort of thing."

"Good. Has he left?"

"Just left, actually. Evey didn't want him to go, so that took some convincing. She gave in the end, though, without a fuss."

"That's good. I'll let you go, though. We're goanna watch a movie."

"Have fun!"

"Thanks, Mom!" Adam ended the call and set his phone on the couch. "All set."

"Did she even question anything?" Ken asked with a wrinkled brow.

"No, just gave in right away." But Adam knew the reason. She was undoubtedly still feeling responsible for his breakdown during the week. He could tell her it wasn't her fault all day, but that wouldn't stop her guilt. *Maybe when I go home tomorrow, I'll talk it out with her. Couldn't hurt to try.*

The three of them spent the rest of the evening watching movies while Cassie clung to Adam more than she had ever done in the past. She was horribly shaken up. Adam didn't say anything to her, but he held her to his side without complaint. Eventually, Ken left Adam and Cassie alone.

Once Adam was sure Ken was busy in his own room, he turned to Cassie. "Why didn't you go home instead of looking for me?"

"I...I," Cassie stuttered, her eyes fearful.

Adam's heart broke. Cassie was always so cool and confident. To see her so broken up was agonizing.

She whispered, "Promise you won't tell anyone."

"Promise," Adam assured her.

Cassie sighed. "There's...a lot...you don't know about me." She took a deep breath and explained, "My birth name was Cassandra Corbant. My family...was the last to live in Corbant Manor."

Adam's eyes widened. He'd thought the Corbant family murders were just a local horror story. It said the father of the Corbant family went crazy and slaughtered his wife, his oldest daughter, their cook, and their maid. Only the youngest daughter escaped, and the father was never found. Never in a hundred years did Adam think he would meet the sole survivor of that horrific tale. "I...I'm sorry."

Cassie shrugged, trembling. She was clearly still haunted by the incident, and Adam didn't blame her. "That's why I'm adopted. It happened when I was three, and I didn't find a family to live with until I was six. Things were fine for a bit, but then..." Cassie paused, shuddered, and bit her lip. "About three years ago...my adoptive father...Kaleb...came into my room at night."

Adam's skin began to crawl, but he asked, "What happened?"

"I fought him off...threatened to tell Darcy...my mother. Ever since, I haven't...I've preferred to be elsewhere," Cassie confessed, her eyes downcast.

"Why haven't you gone to the cops?" Adam asked, horrified.

"They'd take me away. I don't want to go back to an orphanage...," Cassie whimpered with fresh tears in her eyes.

"It can't be worse than...than that." Adam shifted uncomfortably.

"It is the very worst," Cassie assured him. "Besides, I'm even better at defending myself now, and I'll still tell Darcy if he does anything. He won't risk that. Just..." She hesitated a moment before sighing. "Can't you just be happy I felt safer with you?"

"I want you to be safe no matter what."

Cassie smiled. "You're so sweet."

Adam grinned, but he faltered. There were still questions that needed answering. Deciding on the most immediate, he asked, "So...who was that guy?"

"No idea," Cassie said with a shrug.

"None whatsoever?"

"Not a bit."

"Then why was he after you? How did he know your name?"

"Beats me." Cassie shrugged. She looked at a clock on the wall above them and said, "It's getting late."

Adam suddenly remembered how tired he was. The excitement of earlier had temporarily relieved him of his exhaustion, but when he saw the time, it came back in full force. With a sigh, he got up and said, "I'm gonna try to sleep, if that's all right."

Cassie stood with him. "As long as you don't leave me alone."

"Not gonna happen," Adam assured her, taking her hand.

Together, they entered the hallway and turned left to a door beside the opening to the stairs. The bedroom inside was small with no windows. The majority of its space was taken up by a simple full-size bed, an unremarkable three-drawer dresser, and a nightstand with a shade-less lamp sitting on it.

After kicking off their shoes, the pair climbed into the bed and pulled the covers up. Cassie once again latched herself onto Adam's side and laid her head on his chest.

Adam kissed her forehead and closed his eyes, having a moment to consider how lucky he was to have her before sleep took him. Unfortunately, it would not be restful.

In his dreams, Adam found himself naked in a black, empty room. He could see himself as clearly as if a spotlight were shining on him, but there was no source for the light, and as far as he could tell, the only thing in the room was the cold, earthen floor he was standing on.

Then a soft, dry voice broke the silence around him. "I had hoped it would not come to this."

The voice sounded familiar to Adam, though he couldn't remember when or where he'd heard it before. "What are you talking about?" he asked, looking around for the speaker.

"Your will is far stronger than I had expected. Thus, we must speak face-to-face." A shadow moved out of the surrounding darkness. It was a hooded and cloaked figure that towered over Adam. It tilted its head up, and Adam screamed in horror.

The being's face was leering and skull-like, with small thorn-like horns sprouting from around its forehead, its cheeks, and its chin. The dark, grey-blue flesh around its mouth was peeled back, exposing the teeth and muscles beneath. Worst of all, however, were the thing's sunken, coal black eyes. The creature was illuminated in the same way as Adam, but there was a subtle glint in its eyes that reflected part intelligence and part malevolence.

Adam stumbled back and tried to cover himself, but the thing said, "It is of little use. There is nothing of yours that is hidden from me."

"Who are you?" Adam asked, recalling a nightmare earlier that week when he had looked in his mirror and seen that horrible face looking back.

"I have many names," the mysterious figure replied. "My proper name is Asmodeous, but perhaps your histories will remember me as the Dark Master."

"The...The King of Demons?" Adam stammered, his blood chilling. He knew a few demon's names from his horror obsession, but Asmodeous was one he hadn't heard often. He knew enough, however, to suspect that he was in way over his head.

Asmodeous laughed in response. It was cold and mirthless, more menacing than a growl of anger. "That is but a shadow of the truth. There were those who wished to erase me from the world's memory, and so they created an image and a myth to go with my name to diminish and mock me."

"What do you want with me?" Adam asked, though he had already guessed the answer.

"There is much to be done," Asmodeous explained. "Things are in motion that you cannot fathom, but in order to guide them properly, I require a physical form. You will provide this for me."

Asmodeous's words rang in Adam's head. *He wants to possess me.* Did that explain the strange things Adam had been experiencing, or the dreams?

Then Asmodeous said, "Two consciousnesses struggling for control over a single body will create some...unpleasant side effects."

Adam blinked and looked up at Asmodeous. "Why haven't you just taken over completely?"

"As I said, boy, your will is far stronger than I anticipated. Even now, your subconscious mind is pushing back against my presence."

Adam's heart leapt. If his subconscious mind was enough to hold Asmodeous at bay, perhaps he could consciously force him out?

However, Asmodeous laughed in reply to Adam's thoughts. "Don't overestimate yourself, boy. Your will is nothing compared to mine. In time, you will succumb to me whether you wish it or not. It is inevitable. However, you have the choice to make the process much simpler."

"And what do you plan to do with my body?" Adam scoffed, putting on a bold air to try and shake his fear.

"There is far too much for you to comprehend. However, I can offer my word that once my work is complete, you will be returned to full control of your faculties."

Adam was dumbstruck. A demon—the King of Demons, no less—was going to just give him his body back once he'd done whatever he needed to do? It went against everything Adam understood about demonic possession...which admittedly wasn't much, but it was enough to know demons didn't like letting go once they had a hold of someone. "How do I know you'll honor your word? Hell, how do I know any of this is real and not some really messed up dream I'm having?"

Asmodeous studied him for a moment. Adam imagined that if Asmodeous had had lips, he might have smiled.

"It is wise of you to doubt me, boy. However, there is a way I can offer proof of my existence. In the wine cellar of Corbant Manor, behind a shelf on the westward wall, there is a tunnel leading to what was once my prison. Go and see for yourself, and then we shall see if you still believe this to be a dream."

Before Adam could reply, the scene dissolved around him, and he woke up with Cassie lying next to him, just as she had been when he had fallen asleep. Adam bit his lip and looked at her, trying to decide if he believed what he'd heard in his dream or not. Asmodeous's words echoed through his mind, almost as though he were speaking to him at that moment, but it was too ridiculous to believe. Almost.

Was it mere coincidence that Cassie confessed her birth name to him, and then Asmodeous spoke of being imprisoned beneath the mansion? Were the two connected, or did Cassie's revelation spring Asmodeous into being in his mind, and he made up the connection on his own? Was it all just a dream after all?

Adam considered going to see for himself if Asmodeous's words were true, but how would he feel if they were? He'd be confirming that the King of Demons wanted to possess him. *What a comforting thought.* Perhaps it would be better for it to just be a dream and for him to go back to sleep?

At first, Adam did try to rest, but his conversation with Asmodeous replayed in his head over and over again. That horrible face appeared in his mind every time he closed his eyes. What could he do? He had to know for sure. It was the only way to put his mind at ease. If it was all just an elaborate dream, great! If not...Adam preferred not to think about it.

Adam lay in bed for some time, planning his escapade to Corbant Manor. It wouldn't be difficult to get Ken's keys and drive out that way. He'd just have to be extra careful not to get pulled over, which shouldn't be a problem. Once Adam was satisfied with his plan, he started sliding out from under Cassie as gently as he could manage.

However, she stirred awake and looked at him. "Where are you off to?" she asked sleepily.

Adam bit his lip, taken aback by how cute she was in her sleepy state. However, the task at hand weighed heavily on his mind, and he couldn't dwell on her for long. Should he tell her where he was going? *Most likely not.* With how she behaved when she had told her story earlier that evening, Adam guessed telling her he was going to the very place it happened would not go well. So, he lied. "I had a weird dream, and I can't stop thinking about it, so I'm gonna walk around a bit to clear my head."

"I'll come with you." Cassie made to get up from the bed.

"No," Adam said sharply.

Cassie's eyebrows shot up in surprise. Adam took a deep breath and placed a hand on her cheek.

"Don't worry. I just need to be alone with my thoughts for a minute."

Adam hadn't meant to repeat what she had said in the grove earlier. But Cassie seemed to take it for exactly that, her eyes filling with pain.

Guilt tore away at Adam. *She thinks I'm paying her back for earlier.* Cursing his lack of tact, Adam decided he might as well confess. "Look...the dream was about...Corbant Manor. There was something...weird...in the dream, and I...I need to know if it's real or not."

"Don't go," Cassie whispered urgently, her eyes wide and fearful as she grabbed Adam's forearm.

Adam ran his other hand through her hair before pulling away. "I have to know."

"Adam, please don't go!" Cassie pleaded, but Adam shook his head before stepping out into the hallway. If his resolve was going to hold, he had to leave now.

16. Return to House Corbant

Adam crept across the living room to the kitchen. With a pang of guilt, Adam slid Ken's keys off the rack as quietly as he could manage, made his way to the car, and slid inside, hoping against hope that Ken wouldn't hear his car starting. Nervously shaking, Adam slid the key into the ignition and turned. The car's engine sprang to life with a soft purr.

Almost too afraid to move, Adam waited for a minute or two while the car idled, seeing if Ken had been awoken. Once he was certain his friend's slumber hadn't been disturbed, he buckled in and adjusted his mirrors.

Suddenly, the passenger door opened, and Cassie got in beside him.

Adam looked up at her in shock and asked, "What are you doing?"

Cassie stared out the windshield, buckling her seatbelt. "I can't let you go alone." Her eyes were red from crying, but there were no longer tears on her cheeks. Her expression was both haunted and resolute.

Adam placed a hand on her shoulder. "Really...you don't have to do this."

Cassie sighed and bowed her head again, closing her eyes. "I...I can't keep running forever."

"You don't have to face something as horrible as this."

Cassie shook her head. "Yes, I do. Living here in this town again...it's bound to keep getting brought up. I can't keep having a panic attack every time someone mentions it. I...I need to face my demons."

"Are you sure about this?" Adam asked, still unconvinced.

She nodded, her eyes fearful but determined.

Yet her word choice called to mind the dream he'd had before deciding to go to the mansion. Frowning, Adam asked, "Know anything about a demon called 'Asmodeous?'"

Cassie blinked and turned to look at him, frowning. "Where did that come from?"

Adam blushed and turned away, not sure what he was expecting. "Never mind. Then...I guess we're off," he said awkwardly, shifting the car into reverse and pulling out of the driveway.

Cassie rode in silence, her eyes fixed on the road ahead. Adam took it easy on the streets—the last thing he needed was to be pulled over in a car he had stolen, especially without a license.

It didn't take him long to find the driveway entrance at the edge of the Corbant property. The location of the mansion was common knowledge in town. They drove along the cobblestone driveway leading up the hill through the woods, and Adam asked Cassie once more, "Are you sure about this?"

Cassie nodded. "Yes."

Slightly heartened by her affirmation this time, Adam didn't press the matter. After what felt like an eternity, they crested the hill, and the headlights fell upon the wrought iron gate of Corbant Manor, left ajar.

Adam frowned. "You'd think they'd have locked the gates."

Cassie stared at the mansion in silence, her eyes glassy. Adam looked out at it himself as they passed through the gate. It was a looming structure, with high gables and a tower that pierced the moonless night sky. To Adam, it resembled the bastard child of a Victorian mansion and a Gothic castle.

"Did it always look straight out of a horror movie?"

"Pretty much," Cassie replied darkly, her eyes still fixed on it.

It must have been quite impressive in its time, but thirteen years of being uninhabited had left their mark. Shingles had fallen from the roof in some spots, and the yard was unkempt.

Adam scanned the area, noticing another black car parked in the tall grass off to the side of the driveway. "Who could that be?" he asked, craning his neck to get a better look.

Cassie turned to him and asked, "Huh?" He pointed at the car, and she frowned. "Doesn't look familiar."

"Doesn't look too old either," Adam observed.

Cassie shrugged. "At least it doesn't look like a cop." She turned her eyes back up to the mansion, biting her lip. Adam placed a hand on her shoulder, and she heaved a sigh. "Let's get this over with."

Adam didn't argue as he cut the engine. They got out, and together, they walked up the steps to the front wrap-around covered porch. *Literally straight out of a horror film.* A chill ran down his spine, and his eyes darted for a moment to a nearby window, expecting to see a face looking back at him. Thankfully, there was only darkness.

His hand trembling, Adam grabbed the doorknob and turned. The door slid open with an alarmingly loud creak. After a deep breath, he stepped over the threshold with Cassie following close behind. She closed the door, and Adam pulled out his phone, turning on its flashlight.

"I need to get to the cellar. Which way?" Adam scanned the foyer. Stairs on either side of the room ascended to a landing overlooking the entryway. Directly ahead was a doorway to a long hall, and the landing overhead had a similar archway. A wooden angel hung from the landing's railing, its arms spread as if in welcome.

Cassie pointed down the ground floor hallway. Nodding, Adam led the way, his phone at his chest, its beam of light following whichever direction his eyes were turned. The light reflected off the window at the end, startling him at first. The hall was lined with lightless sconces and dusted-over paintings that Adam couldn't make out the details of. They passed two doors opposite each other on the left and right.

Cassie moved closer to him, trembling.

Suddenly, the next door ahead burst open, and a tall, balding man stepped out into the hallway. Cassie screamed and Adam jumped, nearly dropping his phone. He pointed it toward the man, who was leering at them both with wide eyes and a slack-jawed look that made Adam's skin crawl. With a sudden jolt of horror, he recognized Cassie's dad, who had dropped her off on Halloween. He had been unassuming then, but now his eyes were bulging from their sockets, and his mouth twitched unnervingly.

Her dad pulled a shining cross-hilted dagger from his belt and raised it to eye level as he cooed, "Cassie, my little girl...Come to Daddy!"

From behind the door, another man's voice called, "Kaleb, wait! What are you doing?"

Kaleb ignored the other voice and advanced toward Adam and Cassie, his lips lifting into the most nightmarish smile Adam had ever imagined. Adam turned to run, but Cassie was rooted where she stood, her eyes wide in unbelieving horror. Whatever she had expected to face here, her pedophile father had not been it.

With no time to think, Adam seized Cassie's hand and yelled, "Run!" Hand in hand, they darted back down the hallway as Kaleb gave chase.

Adam made for the front door, seized the handle, and turned, but the door wouldn't open. "No!" he cried, throwing himself into it, but it wouldn't budge.

"Forget it!" Cassie shouted, grabbing his arm. They raced up the stairs with Kaleb dashing up the opposite side.

Suddenly, Cassie stopped and doubled back, nearly falling into Adam before slipping by him lithely and seizing his other arm to lead him back down the stairs. When they turned to head back into the hallway, there was a thud overhead, followed by a grunt of pain. Adam hoped it was the sound of Kaleb losing his footing after realizing they'd changed direction. Cassie then pushed Adam through the first door down the hallway to the left, which opened into a short hallway lined with painted portraits.

Cassie pressed her back against the door and whispered very softly, "We're going to need to outmaneuver him if we want to get to the cellar."

"Does that really matter at this point?" Adam whispered back, aghast.

"It might be all that matters at this point." She looked around nervously. "They aren't letting us leave."

"They?"

Cassie nodded, her eyes wide and fearful.

Adam caught a hint of movement from one of the portraits. Shaking his head to make sure he wasn't imagining it, he directed the light toward it. The eyes of a woman in an elaborate dress were fixed on him. He shone the light around the room and found all the other portraits' occupants also staring at him.

Frozen in mounting terror, Adam watched them raise their hands to point at him, their mouths slowly opening and their eyes widening. Then, the gallery was filled with an unearthly shriek. Adam made to cover his ears, but Cassie grabbed one of his hands and led him to a door on the far side of the gallery. The painted eyes and fingers followed them, and the shrieking continued.

The door led into a large parlor filled with dusty furniture. The moment the door was closed behind them, the shrieking stopped.

"What the hell was that?" Adam asked. Corbant Manor had always been the supposedly haunted house in Corbanton, but he had never suspected the stories would be true.

Cassie didn't answer, but instead jerked her head toward a door just down from the portrait gallery entrance. "We can double back through the foyer to get around Kaleb."

Still shaken by what had happened in the gallery, Adam allowed her to lead the way. *They screamed. The paintings fucking* screamed *at me.*

Once again, Cassie stepped into the hallway, but this time, a tall man with dark hair, dressed in jeans and a blue hooded sweatshirt, was coming toward them. Adam recognized him as the man Ken had almost run over. *He must have brought Kaleb here.*

The stranger held up his hands and called, "Wait!"

"You!" Cassie shouted in surprise.

"Cassie, what's going on? Why is Kaleb—Hey, wait! Stop!"

Before the stranger even finished speaking, Cassie pulled Adam back into the foyer, and they raced up the stairs. When they turned to head down the upstairs hallway, Adam saw something that would haunt him for the rest of his life.

Floating almost a foot above the floor was a grotesquely thin and pale woman in a flowing black gown. Her eyes were completely white, and her mouth and chin were smeared with blood. The woman's long arms were spread wide, and countless spiders crawled along the floor, walls, and ceiling around her.

Adam was paralyzed with fear, but Cassie was a step ahead. The woman simply stared as Cassie darted to the first door on the left and pulled Adam in. The room they entered was a hallway like the one directly beneath them, but instead of portraits, there were wooden chairs set against the walls.

Cassie closed the door as quietly as she could manage and whispered, "With any luck, Kaleb has no idea we're in here."

Adam stared at the door, unable to get the image of the floating woman out of his mind. If he blinked, he could still see her white, lifeless eyes staring at him. He imagined any minute the spiders would start creeping under the door.

Cassie gave him a light shake. "Snap out of it!"

"What *is* this place?" Adam asked in a shaky whisper.

"A nightmare." Her eyes darted from side to side before she looked back at Adam again. "We need to get something to defend ourselves with, like a poker from the fireplace or a knife from the kitchen."

Adam nodded, gathering his wits slowly.

Cassie then asked, "What do you need from the cellar?"

Adam took a deep breath. "There's...supposed to be a secret passage on the west wall of the wine cellar."

Cassie nodded. "It ends in a dead end, though, so we'll need to deal with Kaleb first."

Adam nodded. "That makes sense—" he began, but then he lost his train of thought.

Something occurred to him.

Why didn't she question him about the secret passage? More importantly, how did she know it ended in a dead end?

Adam's blood chilled. *She must already know about it, and if she knows about the passage...*

"Let's go!" Cassie whispered urgently, but Adam was unable to move as the horrible truth dawned on him. Cassie grabbed his hand, but he pulled it away. "Adam?" she asked nervously.

He turned to look at her slowly, trembling with barely contained rage. "You...You know about the passage."

"Of course, I know about it. Now let's go get—"

"So, you know about Asmodeous too, don't you?"

"Where...Where is this coming from?" Cassie stammered, backing away from Adam toward the door.

"Answer me!" he demanded, his voice rising.

"Adam, please! Keep your voice down! If he hears—"

Adam cut her off again. "Did you put this demon into me?"

She stared at him, her mouth opening and closing as though words had failed her. "A-Adam...I..." she began, her voice breaking and tears filling her eyes.

Suddenly, the door behind Cassie burst open, slamming into the back of her head and sending her sprawling into a chair beside Adam with a crash. Adam's anger dissolved when Kaleb stepped in. Her dad took a quick glance around before his eyes settled on Cassie's crumpled form on the ruins of the chair.

Horrified, Adam moved to stand between Kaleb and Cassie, but Kaleb pointed the cross-hilted dagger at him and hissed, "Stay out of my way, boy!"

Adam held up his hands in surrender. Kaleb scooped Cassie up onto his shoulder, never taking his eyes off Adam.

"Now, if you'll excuse us, I need to have a chat with my daughter."

As Kaleb stepped past him, Adam caught a glimpse of Cassie's face. Her eyes were half-open and unfocused, and she groaned groggily. Kaleb carried her toward the door on the far side of the room.

Adam moved forward to reach for Cassie, but Kaleb must have heard him. He turned around and brandished the dagger once again. "Stay back, or you'll regret it!"

How could I be so stupid? Adam chastised himself as Kaleb and Cassie passed through the door, leaving it open. Careful not to get too close, Adam followed. The door led to a balcony overlooking the sprawling ballroom. Kaleb was carrying Cassie down a spiral staircase to the floor below. Adam reached the bottom of the stairs as Kaleb was halfway to a door at the back, leading toward the ground floor hallway.

Then another door along that same wall opened, and the stranger came into the ballroom. He took a quick look around and locked eyes with Kaleb. "What the hell are you doing!?"

"Stay out of my way!" Kaleb repeated, pointing the knife at the stranger, who looked on in shock and confusion. Kaleb finished crossing the room, opened the door, and disappeared inside with Cassie.

As though a spell over both of them had suddenly been broken, Adam and the stranger dashed for the door. Adam grabbed the handle as the man rammed it with his shoulder, but something on the other side held it in place.

After another shove, the man backed away. "There's a door on the other side, from the hallway. I'll try that one!" He headed back the way he had come, leaving Adam alone in the ballroom with his hand still on the doorknob.

Adam tried turning the knob again but to no avail. Tears filled his eyes, and he pressed his forehead against the door. This was all his fault. If he had only kept his voice down, Kaleb wouldn't have found them, and they could have dealt with whatever Cassie had done to him after they were safely out of this place. If only he had waited to confront her about it, but the pain had gotten the better of him, and he hadn't been able to control himself.

You can't save her.

The loathsome voice cut through Adam's thoughts like Kaleb's dagger, sending a shiver down his spine.

You can't save her, but I can.

Have you been here the whole time? Adam thought in reply.

I have.

"Then why haven't you stepped in already?" Adam hissed aloud, his pain and anger causing his thoughts to spill from his mouth.

In my current state, my powers are far too limited.

Adam closed his eyes and gritted his teeth. *How convenient.* Still, despite the agony of Cassie's betrayal, Adam couldn't bear the thought of what Kaleb might do to her. If Asmodeous could stop it...but then he would win.

You have the power to save her now, but if you do not act on it, then you are as much to blame for her fate as Kaleb will be.

Adam heaved a sigh, his emotions in a whirlwind as he tried to think. Finally, he said aloud, "How does it work, then?"

17. Unforgivable

Cassie's head was throbbing. One moment, Adam was confronting her, but everything afterward was hazy. She was set down on something hard. It might have been wood, but her mind was so foggy, it was difficult to be sure.

Her vision slowly unblurred. There was a scrape and thud, followed soon by another. She was lying face down on the edge of a crate, her legs dangling to the floor. Shakily, Cassie tried to get up, but the room lurched, and her stomach heaved. She froze, waiting for the room to stop spinning.

The most sickening voice imaginable came from behind her. "You know, I've seen some *very* strange things since coming here."

"Where...Where are we?" Cassie replied, blinking slowly as though it would ease her dizziness.

"The one place in this madhouse where we can have some privacy," Kaleb replied.

Panic suddenly seized Cassie. If she and Kaleb were alone...completely alone...then there was little doubt about his intentions with her. Whatever had happened to him since coming to the mansion seemed to have caused something to snap, and that meant...

Cassie's thoughts stopped dead, and her stomach did cartwheels. She had to fight back! Now!

Cassie made to rise again, but her head was still swimming. Her arms buckled, and she grunted with frustration, trying to will the dizziness away. She propped herself up off the crate on her elbows. Then, a firm hand grabbed her by the back of her neck and forced her face down again.

Cassie immediately latched onto the hand and dug her fingernails into his skin as hard as she could. Kaleb gasped and released her, and for a moment, Cassie thought she might be able to roll away, but then he seized her wrists. She tried to wriggle free, but Kaleb weighed at least twice as much as her and pressed his full weight down on her arms.

He pulled her wrists down toward her lower back, and Cassie flailed as hard as she could to dislodge his grip. She even managed to free a hand momentarily, but he seized it again. Cassie gasped and went limp, the room spinning around her and sapping her strength. Kaleb pinned her wrists to the small of her back, and then he pressed himself against Cassie's backside. She groaned and shuddered in revulsion.

No. Please, no!

Cassie felt her pants slowly being tugged down. Tears spilled from her eyes, and she pleaded desperately, "Daddy...please...Please don't do this to me...Please, Daddy..." She begged until her voice broke into sobs.

Kaleb seemed to freeze for a moment. Then he said softly, "Shhhhh. Don't cry. I just want to love you, my dear."

Cassie could already feel the cold air against her exposed rear. There was nothing between her and him and no one left to protect her. Trembling, her stomach roiling, she gritted her teeth and braced herself for what was about to happen.

Suddenly, there was a tremendous bang followed by a crash. Kaleb gasped, and then he was suddenly pulled away from her in a scream of terror. Cassie immediately pulled her pants back up and turned slowly.

Kaleb was suspended, spread-eagled, in mid-air. Several shadowy tendrils snaking along the walls from the doorway held him up.

Cassie turned toward their source and gasped in awe. Adam stood there, but his eyes had turned entirely black. The bang must have been the ballroom door now lying in splinters on the other side of the room.

Kaleb thrashed and struggled, but the shadows holding him offered no give as Adam walked over to Cassie. He reached out a hand to help her, and she took it. However, when she stood, the room lurched once again. Adam pressed his other hand to her forehead. A bone-chilling cold ran through Cassie's head, and the wooziness was gone. She blinked and looked at him.

"You will want to witness this," Adam said, but it was not his voice.

Savage triumph surged through Cassie. It was the voice of Asmodeous himself.

Asmodeous turned away and walked back out into the ballroom. The suspended and still-struggling Kaleb floated behind him. Once Kaleb crossed the threshold, Cassie looked around for her cross-hilted dagger. *How dare he touch it!* She found it on the floor and grabbed it before following Kaleb and Asmodeous into the ballroom.

They stopped on the other side, but Kaleb slowly floated to the center of the room, rising as he went. Asmodeous's voice boomed as he declared, "We have tolerated your foul presence for long enough."

Feral pleasure surged through Cassie. Kaleb was getting his at last!

Asmodeous turned to her and asked, "Is there anything you wish to say to him?"

"Yes." Cassie took a step forward, her eyes locked on Kaleb. A fresh tendril wrapped around his head, turning it to face her, while another held his mouth shut. His eyes pleaded for mercy, but Cassie thought about what had just nearly happened to her.

Hatred surged through her, and her lips peeled back from her teeth in a ferocious glare. "I fucking HATE YOU!" she shrieked.

Her fingernails dug into her palms as her words echoed in the cavernous room. It wasn't enough. Cassie inhaled a slow, deep breath through clenched teeth before letting loose.

"I wanted a family! I needed..." Tears filled Cassie's eyes, running hot down her cheeks, but not as hot as her blood. "I needed a father, but you...You are..."

Cassie struggled to give voice to all of her hate and resentment.

"You are a fucking monster! You ruined my life, made me hate myself, and tried to fucking rape me! You should have protected me, but instead, you turned me into some sick fucking fantasy!" She paused for a breath and looked into Kaleb's eyes. They still pleaded for mercy, and Cassie almost laughed. "How does it feel to be the helpless one now? How does it feel to be the plaything? How does it feel to know that you fucking deserve this?"

Kaleb grunted in protest and strained against the tendrils binding him. Cassie almost wished she could hear him beg for his life, but no amount of spite would make her ever want to hear his voice again. She smiled—she was about to be free of him, once and for all. *Free at last.*

She closed her eyes, imagining a world without Kaleb in it, and her smile widened. Cassie looked up at him again. Tears spilled from Kaleb's eyes, but Cassie was through with him.

She stepped back and said to Asmodeous, "Make sure he can't come back, just like Sam."

"As you wish," Asmodeous replied.

"One more thing," Cassie turned to look at Kaleb. "Make it hurt. Make him feel how he made *me* feel."

"As you wish." Asmodeous turned his coal-black eyes back toward Kaleb's struggling form. He tilted his head, and another shadowy tendril shot out from his form along the floor. It traced a path to where Kaleb was suspended and then rose up with the others, slithering up toward him like a shadowy snake. It slid under his pants leg, and in the next moment, Kaleb's eyes bulged from their sockets, blood soaking through the crotch of his pants.

More tendrils shot out from Asmodeous and wriggled their way up to Kaleb as Cassie looked on. Kaleb thrashed and choked, blood spewing from his closed mouth, until a tendril ripped open his lips and shot up toward the ceiling.

One by one, in a shower of blood, the shadowy tendrils tore out of his chest, and he was allowed one final choking scream before Asmodeous straightened his head. Every tendril pulled, and Kaleb exploded in a shower of blood and gore.

Cassie did not turn away when Kaleb's blood and viscera fell to the floor. She turned her eyes toward the steaming pile that had once been the man who tried to rape her. Cassie's lip tilted up into the barest hint of a cruel smile. *No less than he deserved.*

Then, Asmodeous said, "Per our bargain," and collapsed.

"Master, wait!" Cassie shouted, but his body had already crumpled to the ground. She dropped the knife and kneeled beside him, unsure of what to do or say. Miraculously, they were both untouched by Kaleb's blood, though the pool was slowly spreading.

Finally, Adam stirred and sat up. Cassie moved to help him, but Adam snapped, "Get away from me."

Cassie backed away as though Adam had slapped her. "A-Adam..."

He slowly climbed to his feet without looking at her. "While Asmodeous was in control, he showed me everything that happened between you two. Everything, Cassie."

Tears filled Cassie's eyes. "Adam...please...I...I'm s-s-so...so sorry..."

"Don't." Adam turned toward the far door leading into the portrait hall. He stood still for a moment before turning his head to the side, his eyes fixed on the floor and his expression unreadable. He then said firmly, "I never *ever* want to see you again."

Cassie quivered, pain welling in her chest. Her heart was breaking. "Adam...please...please don't leave me."

However, Adam ignored her and continued toward the door. Cassie wanted to go after him, but her legs felt far too heavy.

"Adam! Adam, please!" she sobbed. "Adam...please come back! I-I love you!"

Adam paused, her words hanging in the air between them.

Daring to hope, Cassie whispered, "Please...don't go."

However, without looking back, Adam pulled the door open, walked through, and shut it firmly behind him.

Cassie stared at where he had been just a moment ago, her legs buckling. She fell to her knees, clutching at her chest as her tears flowed freely. Cassie bawled her misery to echo from the walls and high ceiling around her.

She had no idea how long she let her pain out, but she eventually got the feeling she wasn't alone. Taking a shaky breath, she turned toward the center door leading into the hallway and saw the stranger appearing shocked and pale. *How much had he seen?*

"You," she hissed, her pain suddenly welling up into rage at the man who had started all of this. If not for him, tonight wouldn't have gone so disastrously wrong. If not for him, Cassie would still have Adam.

She grabbed the knife off the floor and stood up. "This...this is all your fault!" she spat, advancing on the stranger and pointing the knife at him.

The stranger held up his hands and stammered, "I-I swear, I had no idea what he was going to do!"

"Why did you bring him here!?" Cassie half shrieked, half sobbed, taking another step. Her knuckles were white as she raised the knife.

The man took a step back. "I...I just wanted to know what happened that night! When you ran away, I didn't know what else to do, so I knocked on the door, and he and I talked. He said he'd seen some strange things happen around you, and then I suggested that we both might find out more if we came here. I had no idea he was..."

"A fucking *monster*!" Cassie yelled, the knife trembling in her hand. She was almost there now. One quick thrust into his neck, and the man who had cost her everything would pay.

"Cassie...," a somber voice whispered.

Cassie froze, her eyes wide. *Could it be...?*

"Cassie...," the voice whispered again.

She turned toward it, and her breath caught in her chest. Standing just a few feet away was the transparent form of her older sister.

"A-Ally...," Cassie whispered, tears spilling from her eyes once again.

Ally looked exactly as Cassie remembered her. She was dressed in a simple T-shirt, jeans, and a denim jacket with the shoulder torn open. Ally gave her a sad smile before she turned to face the man. "Derek...," she whispered, a ghostly tear sliding down her cheek.

"Ally...," Derek replied, his eyes glistening. "I...I should have gone with you...that night..."

Ally bit her lip before slowly fading away. Cassie stared at where her sister had been as the memories of that horrible night raced through her mind. Derek said nothing.

Without looking at him, Cassie asked, "Do you still want to know what happened that night?"

"Yes," Derek replied softly.

Cassie's lip quivered. *It's time.* For the first time since leaving Corbant Manor thirteen years ago, Cassie told the story of the night her family died. "It began the day Ally didn't come home. She'd told Dad she was staying at Maddy's, and everything seemed fine, but after we all woke up that Saturday morning, Dad started acting strange. I..." Cassie choked as everything replayed vividly in her head. "I don't know...how...or when, but...he killed Mom. Then I...I heard him screaming that...he...he didn't mean to, but then he went quiet. N-n-next I knew, S-S-S-Sam took over his body. I ran, but he...the house...it wouldn't let me leave. He got the m-m-maid and the c-c-c-cook. I hid in the attic. He was going to find me, but then Ally came h-h-home. He went after her but...but she found me first, and we tried to get away. She sent me down the passage in the basement. She told me I'd be safe. Sam chased me, but I touched the sarcophagus, and he...Asmodeous...he came out and destroyed Sam."

Cassie closed her eyes for a moment.

"He…Asmodeous…he asked to live in my shadow. I said yes. He'd just saved me. I thought we were going to meet Ally…and we would l-l-l-leave together, but…she…s-s-s-she was…already…" Cassie couldn't say it aloud. She remembered vividly emerging from the passage and finding Ally lying with her face against the floor in a pool of blood, a knife wound in her back. Her blue eyes had been empty and lifeless, and Cassie had cried then, just as she was crying now.

Derek said nothing as Cassie let her pain out once again. When she could finally speak once more, she concluded, "He…he's looked after me ever since. He's protected me from K-K-K-Kaleb, or anyone else that wanted to…hurt me. It seemed like…like such a small thing…to find him a body of his own. It…it was all he asked of me. That's how we found Adam, and everything was fine…but…but then…"

"You fell in love with him," Derek finished for her.

Cassie nodded, and the pain in her chest welled once again. At last, she looked at Derek. He was looking at the door Adam had left through, his brow furrowed in thought.

"Cassie…," he said softly, "I know he's protected you all these years, but you have to realize, Asmodeous is just using you."

Cassie sighed. "You…You don't understand. Without Adam…he's all I have left."

Derek shook his head. "There are others. Maddy's still out there somewhere…and Bart."

Cassie blinked in confusion. "Who's Bart?"

Derek frowned before heaving a sigh. "I guess you never heard about him. Bart was one of Ally and Maddy's friends. After word came down about what happened to Ally, he had some kind of fit and ended up in a coma at the hospital. He woke up a few months later, but he wanted nothing to do with me. As soon as he could, he moved away.

"As for Maddy, her dad attacked her the night the news about Ally broke, and she ended up killing him, trying to defend herself. After the cops took her, no one knew where she went, but she made a promise to me and to Ally that she would stay alive. Maddy was as stubborn as they came, and she's still out there somewhere. Maybe Bart can even come around if we can find him together."

Cassie thought about all Derek had told her. She remembered Ally's best friend Maddy, who Cassie had admired and wanted to be like, but

Bart...whoever he was, he was probably better off. She shook her head. "He's the only one who never left me. I can't turn my back on him."

"Then...I'm sorry, Cassie," Derek said as he turned away.

"Sorry?" Cassie frowned.

"Someone has to stop him."

"Stop him? No one can stop him! Didn't you see what he did to Kaleb? He's too powerful...If you get in his way, he'll tear you apart."

Derek paused on his way to the door and heaved a sigh. "I know, but...I have to find a way. I can't just let him hurt anyone else."

Cassie bit her lip. "The only people he's hurt are those who have tried to hurt me."

"What about Adam?" Derek countered, glancing back at her, his expression grave.

His name stabbed her in the chest, and Cassie fell silent.

Derek took a deep breath. "There's no telling how many other people will suffer before he's through. If there's a way, I'll find it."

Panic surged through Cassie, replacing the pain. She couldn't let Derek go after Asmodeous!

Cassie still had the knife in her hand.

She took a step forward, raising the knife slowly when Derek turned his back, but then something pushed her. Cassie stumbled, blinking in confusion as Derek reached for the door handle as if in slow-motion. *No!* Cassie raised the knife again and lunged.

Suddenly, Ally was in front of her. She tackled Cassie out of mid-air and pinned her to the floor. The door closed behind Derek.

"No!" Cassie screamed, struggling against Ally's icy-cold grip on her wrists. "I have to stop him!"

"Cassie...don't do it," Ally whispered.

"I have to!" Cassie sobbed, her hand going limp and dropping the knife. "I...I can't fail him! He's...He's all I have..." She broke down into sobs, the ghost of her sister holding her down. By the time Ally let her up, Cassie knew it was too late, and Derek was gone. She was soaked through with Kaleb's blood that had spread all across the floor, but it didn't matter. Cassie had lost Adam, and she had no idea how to save Asmodeous from Derek.

She turned to Ally standing beside her. Ally's voice whispered, "I love you...Cassie..." and then she faded away.

It was too much for Cassie to bear. The pain, the anger, the frustration, and all the misery and sorrow since that terrible night erupted from her in a scream of rage and anguish bringing her to her knees.

How long Cassie sat there, she had no way of knowing, but when she stood up, there was only one thing on her mind: escaping the mansion and any evidence of her involvement with Kaleb's death. She didn't think Derek would be stupid enough to confront Asmodeous after seeing what he had done to Kaleb. If he became a problem later, she had no doubt that Asmodeous would deal with him.

As for her, Cassie was sure she'd be more useful to Asmodeous if no one suspected her of anything. *Useful...*

A coldness settled over Cassie's heart. If Asmodeous was all she had, then she would serve him for the rest of her life. She owed him everything, and she would give him everything in return.

First, she needed to leave the mansion, and for that, she'd need some new clothes. She could take some of Ally's clothes from her room, then stow the bloody clothes in the passage in the cellar. Cassie and Asmodeous had covered it up so the cops wouldn't find it the night her family died, and it would prove her salvation once again now. Then she'd just have to get home and shower before Darcy woke up. If Derek and Kaleb had left Kaleb's house, they had undoubtedly fed Darcy some story about being gone late, which would allow Cassie to do what she needed to do.

The ghost of a smile spread across Cassie's lips. Asmodeous had never been clear about what his ultimate goal was, but every move they had made up until then had felt like a smaller part of a grander scheme. Whenever she had questioned him about it, he had always said that all would become clear in time. Now, Cassie wasn't sure if she cared. As long as he kept punishing those who had wronged her, there was nothing she wouldn't do for him. Whatever his final goal was, Cassie would be there to see it done...by any means necessary.

18. The Shadow Triumphant

Tears streamed down Adam's face the entire drive from the mansion back to Ken's. He struggled to keep from shaking, navigating Corbanton's streets. The whole night had been far too much for him. Asmodeous taking control of his body had been the most violating experience imaginable. It had been as though he were in a dark room, watching everything through his body's eyes—like a movie screen, but in a disconnected way that made him nauseous.

Adam had agreed for Asmodeous to take control to rescue Cassie, but nothing else. Asmodeous had given up control without argument once she was safe, but Adam could still feel him in his mind, undoubtedly occupying the space Adam had been consigned to while Asmodeous was in control. However, he remained silent.

Trying to ignore Asmodeous's baleful, lingering presence, Adam instead turned his thoughts to the real cause of his misery. He had witnessed numerous things he couldn't explain, only to find out that Cassie was at the center of it all.

No, Cassie was the *cause*. If not for her, none of this would have happened.

Adam tried to make himself angry at her to dull the pain, but it only left him longing for earlier that night, when they were cuddled in bed together. Despite himself, if he could have gone back to before he knew what Cassie had done to him, he would have.

Worse still, everything Asmodeous had shown him made it even harder to be angry at Cassie. She had been forced to deal with things no one should have to at any age, and it all started for her at just three years old. There was no wonder why she felt so indebted to Asmodeous, or why she had no hesitation in condemning Adam to be his host. In her eyes, Adam had been just another guy who would take advantage of her.

That still might not have been enough to soothe Adam's anger...if Asmodeous hadn't also shown him how things had changed for her. Whatever Cassie's intentions had been when things began between her and Adam, her feelings for him had become very real. In fact, they were real enough to almost have her betray Asmodeous.

Despite his own sense of betrayal, Adam pitied her. Part of him even wanted to turn around and go back, hold her and comfort her, tell her it would all be all right now...but it was too late.

His thoughts giving him no peace, Adam needed to go home. When he finally got back to Ken's, he went straight to Ken's bedroom. His friend was stretched out shirtless on a tall bed with a wooden frame, breathing peacefully. Adam hesitated before waking Ken up, feeling guilty but unwilling to spend the night in a bed he had shared with her.

He whispered, "Ken, wake up."

Ken shook his head, his eyes scrunching several times before finally opening. "Hmm?" he grumbled.

"Can you take me home? Cassie and I...we're through," Adam whispered, his voice cracking. A fresh wave of tears hit him.

Ken's eyes opened fully, and he sat up. "What? What happened?"

Adam sighed heavily. "I...I don't want to talk about it. I just...need to go home."

"All right, no worries. I'll take you home," Ken assured him, getting out of bed and throwing a shirt on.

Adam was grateful Ken didn't press the matter. He hadn't yet concocted a believable way to explain what had happened that didn't involve something crazy.

"Is she gone already?" Ken asked when they went out to the car.

Adam nodded in silence.

Ken didn't speak again until they were pulling into Adam's parents' driveway. "Are you going to be okay?"

"I...I don't know," Adam admitted. Despite his having been the one to break up with Cassie, his heart ached. He missed how they had been, even if it had only been for show. A part of him would have been happy to go back to blissful ignorance, but the idea of being with her now after what she had done was unthinkable. Adam would never forgive her, no matter how much he loved her. A fresh wave of tears overcame him at the thought. He was forced to admit that he loved her desperately. *If only we could go back.*

Ken didn't ask for any further explanation, but when Adam moved to get out, Ken offered his hand.

Adam took it, shaking it and murmuring, "Thank you."

"If you want to talk, you know how to reach me."

Adam nodded, repeating, "Thank you," then got out of the car. Dawn was still a couple of hours off. He dug out his house key and let himself in, not bothering to be subtle or quiet. His father was already gone for work, and his mother slept like the dead. Evey, on the other hand, would be glad to see him at any hour.

Adam made his way upstairs, forced to admit that, despite his exhaustion, he was not ready to try to sleep yet. His mind would pour over the events and revelations the night had conjured, granting him no reprieve. Once he reached the top of the stairs, he turned and went into Evey's room instead of his own.

Evey was curled up with a stuffed duck nearly as big as she was. Adam sat on the edge of the bed, a soft sigh escaping his lips. He looked at his innocent little cousin, envying her ignorance, with or without her mental illness. In that moment, Adam would have given anything to be eight and carefree again.

Evey's voice broke his thoughts. "You never came home, A. K."

Surprised, Adam replied, "I...I had some things I...needed to take care of." He hoped his vague reply would be enough to placate her curiosity.

Without moving or even opening her eyes, Evey asked, "Like helping grandma get better, like you said?"

Adam's brow wrinkled in bewilderment. "What are you talking about?"

"Monday night," Evey explained quietly, sleepily turning to look at him. "When you came into my room, you said you'd help grandma, but you would need my help too. When I asked what you wanted me to do, it was like you forgot."

Adam stared at her, unsure of what he was hearing. He remembered the incident very clearly, but he had thought he was sleepwalking. Then the terrible truth occurred to him. *It was Asmodeous. He's setting Evey up to be just like Cassie.* The images Asmodeous had shown him while he was in control flashed through Adam's mind, and it all became clear. Asmodeous got people to do what he wanted by doing things for them no one else could. Once they were in debts they could never hope to pay, Asmodeous had them.

Not her, Adam thought, tears filling his eyes. *She's been through enough.*

Perhaps you could offer an alternative?

Adam took a deep breath. *Checkmate.* Evey had been Asmodeous's ace in the hole if the mansion ordeal went sour...which it had. *Or had it?*

Why else had Asmodeous exposed all of Cassie's secrets to him, if not for him to realize Evey was being set up to be her successor? The elaborate nature of the scheme made Adam's head spin, but he couldn't deny he'd been outplayed. From all he had learned that night, one thing had been made clear: if Asmodeous didn't get what he wanted, people suffered.

Not her, Adam thought again. *On that condition. Leave her out of whatever you're planning, and you can have me.*

As you wish, so shall it be.

Adam looked into Evey's hopeful eyes. She had been waiting patiently for his answers while he argued with himself. So far, Asmodeous had been true to his word, but would he be this time? Unable to think of anything else to say, he stood up.

"I'll do what I can, Evey. I promise."

Unable to face her for what might be the last time, Adam turned away and went to his room. *And your promise to heal Grandma?*

Do not overreach, boy.

You told her you would!

That was before you demanded I leave her out of my plans, but... Asmodeous's voice trailed off thoughtfully.

Adam waited, biting his lip.

It would be far easier to uphold our bargain if Evelyn were returned to your grandmother's care. Very well, it shall be done.

Wait, really? Adam had to admit, he hadn't expected Asmodeous to give in so easily.

In the end, it suits us all better if it is so.

But you most of all, Adam thought with a combination of shame and disgust.

Last chance, boy. The offers have been dealt.

Though his words were impatient, Asmodeous's tone was as emotionless as ever. *He already knows the answer. He's just waiting for me to say it.*

Adam took a deep breath and sat on the edge of his bed, tears in his eyes. His thoughts turned to his friends—Ken, Walter, Damien, and Lex. He hadn't had a chance to say goodbye, but maybe that was best. *High school friends drift apart eventually anyways.* The thought did nothing to ease the hollow feeling welling in Adam's chest.

Then Adam's thoughts turned to his family. His mom and dad were facing a lot of uncertainty right now, but at least his mom wouldn't have to add losing her mother to it all. Evey would go back to live with her, and the house would almost return to normal, at least until his mom got her job back.

Finally, Adam thought of Cassie. *She never stood a chance.* Unlike Evey, no one had been left to protect Cassie when Asmodeous had gotten his claws into her. Whether by circumstance or by design, Cassie was doomed to be bent to Asmodeous's will. Her falling for Adam had been the first and only thing she had done that hadn't aligned with Asmodeous's wishes, so maybe there was hope that eventually she would be free of him. *Maybe...*

Despite her part in what was about to happen, Adam only wanted the best for her. His time with her had been the happiest of his life, and maybe someday, she'd have a piece of that happiness for herself.

Adam closed his eyes until the afterimage of his walls faded away. He took a deep breath and let it out slowly, savoring the familiar scent of his room one last time before whatever came next. Time was meaningless, and Asmodeous was nothing if not patient, but Adam couldn't wait any longer for the end.

It was time.

I'm ready.

19. Reunion

Cassie woke up Sunday morning to Darcy frantically shouting into her phone. Annoyed, Cassie tried shutting out the noise with a pillow over her head, but Darcy's shrill, panicked voice cut straight through.

Then Darcy was pounding on her door. "Cassie! Cassie!" she nearly screamed.

"What?" Cassie replied groggily, trying to hide her annoyance.

"Let me in, please!"

"All right, just a second," Cassie grumbled, slipping out of bed and heading for the door. She unlocked it and opened it to find a very disheveled Darcy still in her nightgown. Her eyes were nearly bulging from her head. "Have you seen your father?"

Cassie blinked. "Umm...I've been in bed..."

"Your father never came home last night!"

Cassie summoned her best acting skills, pretending to shock herself awake. "Wait, what?"

Darcy nodded and bit her lip. "He said he was going out with a friend for some drinks and not to wait up for him, but when I woke up, he still wasn't home. That's not like him at all!"

"Have you called the cops?" *Like they'll ever find him.* It took all of Cassie's effort to not show any hint of smugness.

"Yes! I've been on the phone all morning, but they won't take it seriously! They said he hasn't been gone long enough!"

Darcy then started pacing up and down the hallway, dialing on her cell phone again. Seconds later, she was on the phone with one of Kaleb's colleagues, asking if they'd seen him. Cassie stifled a groan of annoyance. *You'd freak out over him not coming home one night but never paid enough attention to realize that you had married a fucking pedophile?* She didn't know whether to laugh or throw up.

Her plan the night before had gone off without a hitch, but Darcy's behavior was ridiculous. A part of her wanted to strangle her adoptive mother, but she had gone through the trouble of disposing of evidence last night to avoid that kind of situation with the cops. *Patience. Always patience.*

To Cassie's disgust, she wasn't allowed to leave the house for the rest of the day. Darcy called everyone she could think of in a desperate attempt to locate Kaleb. Each time Darcy got off the phone, she would scream, "Where is he!" Every time, Cassie fought the urge to burst out laughing, though whether out of disgust or amusement, she couldn't tell. When evening came, the police showed up.

Darcy gave her statement, and a cop came to interview Cassie. "Hey, mind if I ask you a few questions?"

Cassie feigned worry. "Is my dad okay?" *Puke.*

"That's what we're going to find out, honey. Now, are you ready to answer some questions?"

Cassie nodded and swallowed fake tears.

"Where were you yesterday around this time?"

"In the woods across the street. I like to go there to think."

"Were you with anyone?"

"No," Cassie answered without thinking. *Best not to give them a reason to go talk to Adam.*

"What time did you come home?"

Cassie acted like she was trying to recall a particularly hazy memory. "It was late, but it couldn't have been too late. Mom wasn't home yet."

"Was your dad still here when you got here?"

"No, he wasn't home."

"Was this unusual?"

Cassie shrugged. "Sometimes his work runs late, or he goes out with friends afterwards. I just...I guess I just assumed..." She let a few tears fall for effect.

The cop patted her shoulder. "It's all right. We'll do everything we can, I promise you. We *will* find him."

The cop finished taking her statement and walked away. Cassie almost smiled with wicked glee. *No, you won't.* The only way anyone would know to look for Kaleb at the mansion is if Derek or Adam talked, but how could they explain the manner of Kaleb's death? The impossibility of what happened would undoubtedly keep them both silent, and Cassie allowed herself the hint of a satisfied smirk. She thought of Kaleb's lifeless meat molding away, never to be seen by anyone ever again.

However, her moment of exultation was cut short when the cops left and she was alone with Darcy once again. Darcy sat in the parlor, sobbing hysterically and hugging a pillow. Cassie sat in the dining room, still contemplating murdering her adoptive mother. She was so pathetic, and to think she had been completely blind to Kaleb's intentions with Cassie. As far as she was concerned, Darcy was no better than Kaleb.

As Darcy cried herself to sleep in her chair, Cassie sat and stared at her with nothing but pure, unadulterated hatred. Eventually, she got up from the dining room table and went to bed, but sleep would be a long time coming. Instead, Cassie spent most of the night staring at her beloved, spotless dagger on her nightstand, fantasizing about driving it into Darcy's skull.

MONDAY MORNING FOUND Cassie in a foul mood. She had not been looking forward to the return to school. The news would have gone crazy over word of Kaleb's disappearance. She would have to act worried or scared all day, and the idea made her ill. At least her miserable attitude would be more convincing since she wasn't happy to be there at all.

Without making eye contact with anyone, Cassie went straight to her first class and sat alone. As she stared at her desk, she pondered just how many times she'd have to cry throughout the day to convince people she gave a shit about her pedophile father being little more than rotten beef jerky by now.

"Is this seat taken?" a familiar voice asked beside her.

Cassie turned, snapping out of her thoughts. Adam sat down next to her.

Stunned, Cassie replied, "No."

Adam stretched out, closed his eyes, and inhaled deeply, as if savoring the smell of the classroom.

Puzzled, Cassie said, "I thought you never wanted to see me again."

Adam chuckled, not opening his eyes. "Come on, Cassie. You know me better than that."

"Then what changed your mind?"

Adam turned to look at her, his eyes entirely coal black. He smiled and whispered in a voice that made Cassie's heart do a backflip. "A great deal has changed, Cassandra."

Cassie's face split into a wide grin. Just as she knew he would, Asmodeous had won. Cassie wanted to punch the air and whoop in triumph. She couldn't remember the last time she had been so happy. It took all of her self-control to remain in her seat and whisper to him calmly, "It's good to have you back, Master."

20. The Girl No More

"Ladies and gentlemen, friends and family, teachers and staff, and most importantly, fellow graduates, it is my honor and my privilege to stand before you all as valedictorian of Corbanton High School's graduating class of 2011," Asmodeous declared from behind the podium. Two years had passed since Asmodeous had claimed Adam's body for his own, and now Cassie sat in the front row of her graduating class in the school gymnasium. The assembly burst into applause and cheers, and Asmodeous waited politely for them to subside.

"You know," one of her fellow graduates said from behind Cassie, "that could have been you if you weren't such a whore."

Cassie turned to look at the speaker, giving them a sultry smile. "You're just upset that you could never afford me, darling." Who the heckler was didn't matter. Cassie had heard the same thing a thousand times before, each time from someone who meant nothing to her, and this was no different. With a flip of her hair, Cassie turned back to face Asmodeous and cheered louder still.

"Thank you all, but it hasn't been without its hardships. High school is a formative part of our lives but is also, most importantly, a transition. A time of change," Asmodeous continued, and the applause died down.

As he spoke, Cassie smiled smugly. *Change indeed.* Ever since Kaleb's death, Cassie had found the fear forcing her to cover herself over the years had melted away, and she took both pride and pleasure in dressing however she wanted...which was usually provocatively. No matter what she wore, guys still tried to come onto her, so she had learned to express herself in whatever way she wanted—no one seemed to care anyway.

"None of us are the same person we were when we first walked into this school four years ago. Some of us learned new things or discovered new talents. Others made new friends or learned to let go of pasts that held us down," Asmodeous continued.

Cassie almost laughed aloud. Asmodeous was describing her experience since coming to Corbanton High School almost to the letter.

"Together, we have laughed, we have cried, we have worried, and we have celebrated. All of us have had experiences that have defined us within these walls. However, today...Today is our greatest triumph yet."

Cassie almost snorted at Asmodeous's words. Her greatest triumph had been seeing Kaleb's shredded corpse lying steaming on the floor of the Corbant Manor ballroom. As Cassie had expected, no one ever thought to look for Kaleb's remains at the mansion. Even if they had, Asmodeous had thoroughly cleansed the ballroom of any evidence of Kaleb, and so his disappearance remained unsolved. Even better, once Cassie turned eighteen, she inherited the property herself and the nearly forgotten family fortune that went with it.

"We will make mistakes in the years to come. We will stumble, and we will fall, but no matter what, we must always rise again."

Cassie's smile faltered for a moment when she thought of her adoptive mother. *She certainly isn't picking herself up any time soon.* Darcy had dissolved into a shell of her former self, turning to drinking heavily and passing out on the couch. As far as Cassie was concerned, Darcy could drink herself to death, and Cassie wouldn't bat an eye.

"Time will continue to move on, and though many of us may never cross paths again, the memories, the lessons...all that we learned and experienced here will define us for the rest of our lives."

At Asmodeous's words, Cassie's smile nearly vanished. He seemed to be referencing Adam's former friends—Ken, Lex, Walter, and Damien. Despite Cassie urging him to do otherwise, Asmodeous had done nothing to maintain those ties of friendship. He had insisted it would be best if they simply parted ways, even though he and Cassie made efforts to keep up the pretense of being in a relationship. They even continued the Saturday training sessions. With Asmodeous in a body of his own, Cassie was learning far better than if he were simply whispering instructions in her ear.

The rest of their time together was focused on staying on top of their classes. Cassie hardly cared, but Asmodeous insisted on making Adam valedictorian. She could only guess why, but it was not her place to question his actions or motives.

"For four years, many of us have thought only of this moment: the moment we get the chance to finally say, 'we did it.' Now that it is here, I say to you all: don't let it end here. Never stop growing. Never stop learning. Never stop adapting, and most importantly, always give yourself a new challenge to meet. Whether it's as simple as earning that first paycheck and getting into a prestigious college, or as grandiose as becoming an entrepreneur or pursuing a career, never lose sight of your goals. Never stop striving. Never stop learning, and remember: this is just the beginning."

Asmodeous's speech concluded, and the assembly burst into raucous applause. Cassie watched Asmodeous shake hands with teachers on the stage. They all congratulated him professionally, but Cassie could tell that he unnerved them. Though Asmodeous had done a tremendous job of adopting Adam's speech patterns and mannerisms, his untold intellect spilled out sometimes, leaving many baffled and sometimes intimidated. The teachers spoke highly of him, but Cassie was certain they at least sensed something amiss.

Still, no one confronted either of them on the subject. Adam's family hugged and sobbed over him for his achievements. All of them, even many Cassie hadn't yet met, were gathered there, except for his grandmother and Evey. After Asmodeous took over, Adam's grandmother had miraculously recovered, and so Evey moved back in with her. Cassie had seen her regularly since but was sad she couldn't be there because of all the noise and the crowds.

Adam's mother insisted on picture after picture of him and Cassie together. Cassie tried not to shudder when Asmodeous put his arm around her waist for one photo, assuring herself he was only doing it to maintain the pretense. *It's Asmodeous, not Adam. Adam is gone.* Then, Taylor finally fought her way through the crowd and threw her arms around Cassie.

Cassie hugged her tightly, savoring the feeling of their bodies pressed together and all the memories it stirred. Though she and Asmodeous had maintained their ruse of a relationship, it was devoid of any real affection or intimacy. To fill that void, Cassie had turned to Taylor. They had developed a close friendship for a year after Asmodeous's triumph before Cassie made her move.

To her delight, Taylor had confessed she wasn't opposed to the idea, and with assurance that "Adam" was okay with it, the two of them had become extremely intimate. In fact, successfully seducing Taylor had boosted Cassie's confidence like nothing else before. They ordinarily kept their relationship pretty under wraps, but now that they might not see most of the people in that gymnasium ever again, Cassie didn't care if their embrace came across as more than just friendly. After a few more pictures with Taylor, Cassie and Asmodeous made to leave the gymnasium.

Lex called to Asmodeous from the crowd.

Cassie ignored him at first, but when Asmodeous turned to face him, she did the same.

Lex walked up, his brow furrowed in anger. "Do any of your friends matter to you anymore?" he demanded.

Asmodeous answered calmly, "You did at one point."

"What's that supposed to mean?" Lex snapped.

Cassie was surprised his tone didn't turn heads, but amidst the commotion of families and graduates, no one seemed to have noticed.

"It means that we as friends had our time, but all times must pass," Asmodeous said simply.

Lex seemed visibly stunned. He looked at Cassie for a moment, his eyes narrowing. She stared back unflinchingly, keeping her expression vague. Then Lex returned to Asmodeous and said, "We'd been friends for a long time before she came along. I thought that meant something to you, but I guess I was wrong. You changed, and not for the better."

Asmodeous raised an eyebrow before stating coldly, "The boy you knew is gone, Alexander. Best you forget him." Leaving Lex stunned into silence, Asmodeous walked out with Cassie in tow.

Once they were in Cassie's car in the parking lot, Cassie turned to him. "Don't you think that was a little bold, using his name like that?"

Asmodeous stared out the window, his face expressionless. "It is in our best interest if these friends of his do not pursue us any further. At last, we can begin our true work."

Cassie started the car and backed out of the parking space. "But what is our true work? After all these years, you still haven't told me."

"All will become clear in time, child. There are steps we must take to prepare, but I assure you that you will not be left in the dark forever."

Though frustrated by his lack of an answer, Cassie trusted him implicitly. "I understand," she replied calmly as they left the parking lot.

LATER THAT EVENING, Cassie reclined on the fallen tree in her grove. She had dropped Asmodeous off at Adam's parents' house, then gone to Darcy's to change into shorts and a tank top before coming here. Despite Kaleb's blissful absence, Cassie still preferred the grove to the house. The woods had always given her peace, and so she retreated to them once again.

She closed her eyes and listened to the sounds of the evening, her hands behind her head and one leg outstretched, the other swaying gently, dangling over the side of the tree.

"Am I interrupting?" Asmodeous's true voice came from below her.

Cassie sighed softly. "Never, Master." She found she preferred it when Asmodeous used his actual voice over when he used Adam's, but he only did it when they were completely isolated.

"Good, because there is something that I must tell you."

Cassie sat up and jumped down from the tree, landing almost directly in front of him. "What's that?" she asked.

"I am leaving."

Cassie had known this was coming sooner or later, but she still didn't like it. She closed her eyes momentarily, trying not to think of dealing with Adam's friends alone. "Where are you heading?"

"There are many places I must visit in order to set things in motion. I may not return for some time."

"Can't I come with you?" Cassie asked, already sure of the answer, but what did she have to lose?

"No, child," Asmodeous said firmly.

Two years ago, Cassie would have nearly gone into a panic attack at the idea of Asmodeous leaving her indefinitely. Now, however, she had had two years to prepare for the news. "What am I to do while you're gone?"

"Tend to the house. We will need it when I return."

Cassie sighed. He was still obsessed with Corbant Manor. There was an edge to her voice that surprised even her as she asked, "Why do you need that house so badly?"

Asmodeous raised an eyebrow. "There are several reasons, but those are not yet your concern."

Cassie wanted to argue that she had a right to know since the house belonged to her, but she bit her tongue. Arguing with Asmodeous was pointless. At last, she bowed her head. "As you say, Master. When will you return?"

"Eventually, I assure you," Asmodeous stated, turning to walk away.

"Wait!" Cassie called.

Asmodeous looked over his shoulder at her, raising his eyebrow yet again. "Yes?"

Cassie had called to him as a knee-jerk reaction to him walking away. Her eyes widened, and she fumbled for something to say, unsure of why she had even called in the first place. But then she remembered.

It looked just like that night...the last time I saw Adam. Bowing her head once more to hide the pain in her eyes, Cassie instead said, "I hope your journey is fruitful, Master."

Asmodeous stared for a moment, his eyes unreadable. At last, he said, "As do I." Then, he turned and continued walking away.

Cassie watched him until he stepped past a tree, and he was gone. She stared at the path he had taken, hoping to see him walking back toward her, but was disappointed to find herself completely alone. Cassie climbed back up the tree and resumed the position she had been in before Asmodeous had come.

She closed her eyes, tears slowly slipping down her cheeks. Whether out of shame or misery, she couldn't tell, but two years had not made the pain any easier.

At first, she had been overjoyed to have Asmodeous back, but her heart still belonged to Adam, no matter how hard she tried to fight it. Seeing him but having it not *be* him had been a kind of agony Cassie couldn't put into words.

With a scream of frustration, Cassie buried her face in her hands. If only Asmodeous had taken her with him. Neither the idea of going home to Darcy's pathetic binging, nor to Corbant Manor to be surrounded by her dead relatives, was very appealing to Cassie. She needed a change of scenery, if only for the night.

Then she got an idea. Her inheritance had included a fairly hefty sum of money. She could withdraw some and take the train to Chicago. Surely, she could find something there to get her mind off her own misery for a while.

Relieved at finally coming up with something to do, Cassie leapt from her branch and headed for her car in the driveway of Darcy's house. As she got in, however, she paused. *Should I invite Taylor along?* A girls' night out could be fun, and Cassie more than liked the idea of them getting a hotel room together and really getting busy. However, it would be difficult for Cassie to hide the real reason she was wanting to get out of Corbanton for a night, and Taylor was observant enough that she would ask questions.

No, it'll just be easier if I go alone.

EARLY THAT EVENING found Cassie on the train to downtown Chicago. Most of the ride she spent on her phone, looking for possible destinations to spend an evening. However, after the train made a stop at some station she wasn't paying attention to, she got the feeling of being watched. Lowering her phone slightly, Cassie scanned the train with her peripheral vision, expecting to find a pervert's hungry eyes staring back.

However, Cassie was pleasantly surprised. Everyone on the train seemed to be trying to avoid eye contact, except for a tall, slender woman in a sparkling violet cocktail dress and a brown fur coat. Curious, Cassie turned to look back, but the woman didn't look away. In fact, she offered a subtle smile that intrigued Cassie. The woman had long, dark brown hair, pale blue eyes, and a feline shape to her face that gave her an air of both elegance and cunning.

The woman got up and walked over to sit next to Cassie. "Do you mind, darling?" she asked with a flutter of her eyelashes. Her voice was silky, sending a pleasant shiver down Cassie's spine.

"Nope," Cassie replied simply, both intrigued and on guard.

"I've never seen you on here before. First trip to the city?"

Cassie nodded, being cautious. The women didn't seem bothered, however.

"Business or pleasure?"

Cassie bit her lip. Her thoughts returned to Asmodeous leaving her in the grove, which in turn reminded her of when Adam had left, and the pain in her chest thrummed threateningly. With a sigh, Cassie replied, "Just looking to get away for an evening, I guess."

The woman's expression softened. "I can understand that. Any idea where you're going to go?"

Cassie shrugged. "I've been looking around, but...I can't decide on anything. I'm..." Cassie caught herself, but the woman waited expectantly for her to finish. She whispered, "I'm only nineteen."

The woman nodded and whispered back, "That does limit your options a bit."

Cassie shrugged. "Any suggestions?"

"Glad you asked," the woman said with a wink that caused Cassie's pulse to rise just a hair. The train was slowing down as they arrived at their destination. The woman reached into a black leather purse under her arm and pulled out a business card. "You can find me here if you like. Tell them you're Lavender's guest when they ask for ID, and you won't have a problem getting in."

Cassie took the card and looked at it. There was an image of the woman on it with her back toward the camera, wearing her fur coat. She was looking over her shoulder with a "come hither" smile. Then Cassie read the information on the card: *The one and only Lavender Mist, only at Forbidden Desires Strip Club.* Cassie looked up at her, her brow furrowed in confusion. "You're a...stripper?"

Lavender simply smiled an exact copy of the smile on her card. "Come visit and find out for yourself."

"And they'll just...let me in? Don't I need to be twenty-one?"

Lavender chuckled musically. "It's a dry club, love. You're old enough already. Just remember: Lavender's guest." With a wink, Lavender got off the train.

Cassie waited for the disembarking crowd to thin while she stared at the business card. Being surrounded by men drowning in their own lust hardly sounded like a good time, but then she recalled Lavender's sultry smile and her alluring wink. A shudder ran down Cassie's spine. *Might not be a bad idea after all.*

Once Cassie was off the platform and somewhere she could step out of the crowd, she pulled out her phone again and searched for Forbidden Desires

Strip Club. It was a few blocks away, but Cassie had walked farther in a single night.

The streets were far more crowded than even Valpo had been. With so many people, Cassie felt a sense of anonymity that was comforting. Like the train, everyone avoided eye contact and went about their business without a care for anything happening around them.

However, as Cassie neared her destination, the crowds thinned. Still, she felt no unease and continued on her way, even as the sky overhead turned to full dark. A neon sign ahead over the door of a brick building declared it to be Forbidden Desires. Nerves crept up on Cassie, but she had come too far to turn back now. She took a deep breath, followed by a step toward the club.

"Nice night for a walk, ain't it?" a man called from behind her.

Cassie whirled around. A tall man with a thick leather jacket, jeans, and biker boots crossed the street toward her. His hair was buzzed short, and his eyes were dark.

Cassie's guard went up immediately. "So what if it is?"

"On your way to work, eh?" the man asked with a smirk that was all too familiar to Cassie.

"Actually, no," she said simply, carefully measuring the distance between the man, her, and the doors of the club.

"Could've fooled me. A pretty thing like you could make millions working at the club."

"Walk away. Now," Cassie stated firmly, readying to flee or fight.

The man looked taken aback. "Snappy little broad, aren't you?"

"Push your luck and you'll find out just how snappy I can be," Cassie countered, moving toward the club without turning her back to the man.

The man put his hands up disarmingly, but then someone from behind tried to grab Cassie by the arms. Before his grip could even tighten, she threw her elbow back, whirled around to punch him in the face, and was back to facing the first man prior to the second even hitting the ground. Though she took satisfaction in the shock in his eyes, she needed to get out of this situation fast.

Cassie chanced a glance over her shoulder. Three more men were closing in down the sidewalk. *Fucking creeps.* However, there was an alleyway nearby that she could dart into and hopefully circle back to make her escape.

Before the other three got any closer, Cassie sprinted down the alley. For a moment, she thought she had gotten away, but then she found the other end blocked by two more men. *Did they set up some sort of fucking ambush?* Panic gnawed at her, but she took a deep breath and rotated on the spot to take stock of the situation. *Four behind, two in front.* Her path was clear.

Cassie lunged as one of the two pulled a gun. However, before he could even aim, she was upon him. She grabbed his wrist and threw her shoulder into his mid-section, knocking him to the ground and snapping his wrist. The man screamed in pain, and the gun fell from his limp hand. Cassie kicked it away before launching herself at the second man barring her path. However, he was ready for her. He swung at her before she made contact, and she slid to duck under him, almost losing her balance. Two from the group behind her came rushing in, but Cassie threw herself to the ground and spun her legs into the air, hitting all three attackers by surprise.

As her assailants stumbled back, Cassie leapt to her feet and lashed out with a series of punches and kicks. The three men retreated against her onslaught, and Cassie saw her chance. Triumphant, she dashed for the mouth of the alleyway without looking back.

Bang! Bang! Bang!

Cassie felt the pain before she heard the gunshot. The three bullets knocked the breath from her, and she fell forward onto the pavement. *What? How?* Cassie's mind was in overdrive.

She heard the first man's voice over her. "Fucking bitch! I'll show you to give me the cold shoulder!"

However, his companions seemed to be panicking. They shouted, "Fuck man, you killed her!" and "Holy shit!" and "Are you insane!"

"Come here," the man grunted, grabbing Cassie by the shoulder and flipping her over.

Cassie had lost control of her body entirely. It trembled and convulsed as the man undid his belt.

"The last thing you're gonna feel is my cock in your pussy, bitch. Teach you to fuck with me!"

No! Not like this! Cassie weakly raised her arms, but her head was swimming. She coughed, her chest feeling far too tight. Tears fell from the sides of her eyes. All her life had been spent dodging situations like this, but it seemed her luck had finally run out. *Someone, help me, please!*

A voice from a man outside her field of vision made her attacker pause. "Steven, this time you have gone too far." The speaker's voice was deep, with a thick eastern European accent.

"Who the fuck are you?" the man who must have been Steven snapped back.

"I am your worst nightmare. Now get away from that poor girl, and if I ever see your face anywhere near my club again, you'll be scooping it up off the sidewalk."

Steven raised the gun again as if in slow motion, but in the next second, a man appeared beside him and grabbed his arm with a grip hard enough to make the thug wince in pain. The man was dressed in a long black overcoat covered with shining buttons and elaborate embroidery, as well as a top hat. He was darkly olive-skinned, with a black circle beard and long, black hair. His pale blue eyes blazed menacingly as Steven cowered before him.

The stranger released his arm and growled, "Run."

Steven immediately turned and ran in the direction he had come.

The newcomer watched him go for a moment, looked around to see if the coast was clear, then kneeled beside Cassie. "I am sorry I did not arrive sooner, my dear. It is a pity you will be dead long before an ambulance arrives, but at least I could allow you to die with some dignity."

The man stood up and pulled a phone from a pocket in his coat.

"Wait!" Cassie choked.

The man looked back down at her, his eyes full of sadness and pity. She coughed. The trembling was easing, but she was rapidly losing feeling throughout her body. Even her vision was starting to cloud over, but she fought with all of her will to stay conscious.

She gasped, "Don't...leave me."

The man heaved a sad sigh. "I will stay with you, then...until the end."

Cassie coughed again, a snarl of frustration escaping her as she fought with all of her might. "I...I don't..." She clenched her teeth and tried to blink the haze away, tears spilling from her eyes. "I...I don't want...to die!"

The man's lip trembled for a moment. "My dear..."

"Please!" Cassie pleaded with a gasp, grabbing at the man's coat, but her fingers were too weak to get a grip on him. *Not like this!*

The man looked at her fallen hand for a moment before gazing back at her face. Cassie could feel herself slipping away.

"Not...like this...," she gasped.

The man took a deep breath. "As you wish."

Epilogue: Pieces of the Past

Asmodeous left Cassie's grove and closed his eyes. A cold sensation descended on his entire body for a moment, and he heard a cacophony of whispers and distant screams. However, both the feeling and the sounds vanished when he opened his eyes, confirming his arrival at his destination.

Enormous trees surrounded him, turning the already dark night into pitch-blackness. Though his eyes could see the outlines of the objects around him, he picked up a fallen limb nearby and ran his hand over the top. At his unspoken command, it burst into flames, providing him with a torch to light the area.

Asmodeous turned his gaze to the ruins ahead. It had been a well-fortified castle at one point, but he imagined it hadn't seen use in more than five hundred years. It was unlikely that many even knew of its existence.

He walked up to the front gates slowly. The portcullis was lowered, but a hole was torn through the bars large enough for a man to slip through unhindered. He ducked through it and surveyed the ruined courtyard. The battlements of the outer wall were crumbling and treacherous. The main keep was not any better off. A single tower that had been the highest point of the keep had collapsed completely, and a section of the walls was cracked entirely in half.

Asmodeous surveyed the remnants of the castle, and memories of the battle flashed through his mind. He climbed the staircases and could almost hear voices shouting in Norwegian, Romanian, or Latin. Asmodeous could almost hear the clash of steel against steel. He could almost see the bodies piling up at the base of the battlements as the slaughter unfolded. Thousands had died that day, many by his own hands. As to what became of their remains, Asmodeous hadn't a clue.

He passed through the cavernous entrance hall to the audience chamber. This was the last room he had been in before his imprisonment. The memory of the titanic battle that took place there replayed vividly in his mind. He could almost feel the energy coursing through him, remembering lashing out at eight attackers with all the power he could muster. It had been he who had rent the walls of the keep asunder, but despite his unquestionable might, he had not been victorious, and the battle had ended with his enemies trapping him in the sarcophagus that had ended up beneath Corbant Manor.

Asmodeous walked up to the crumbling stone chair that had served as his throne. The hair on the back of his neck stood on end. So mighty was the sorcery he had unleashed during that great clash that its echo remained even five hundred years later.

Now, to piece together what transpired after my imprisonment.

Asmodeous sat on the ruined throne and closed his eyes. He extended his unseen senses into the very foundations of the castle and the forest around it, letting his consciousness sift through the residual energy remaining from that fateful day. There was a great deal to assess, but time mattered little to him. He had waited five hundred years, so however long it took for him to find the trail he needed was of no concern.

For a whole week, Asmodeous did not move. Sustained by the power of Asmodeous's own immortal soul, Adam's body no longer required sleep or wholesome sustenance. He let the flow of the energy surrounding the area ebb and recede naturally, searching for the threads of the past. There had been those who had survived the battle, and he had every reason to believe they had remained loyal to him. The echo of their flight from the castle was faint but still present.

One was Elias, a telltale signature Asmodeous couldn't have missed if he had wished it. The other was Cecilia, who Asmodeous himself had trained to control her burgeoning capabilities. The barest hint of a smile crossed Asmodeous's lips, as faint as the emotion conjuring it.

At midday on his eighth day at the castle, Asmodeous was satisfied with the information he had gathered. He stood from the throne and traced Elias and Cecilia's path. They had fled the keep through a secret underground passage, just as Asmodeous had instructed them to do if the battle went ill. Though others failed him, neither Elias nor Cecilia were ever among them. If fate favored him, he would find out what became of them.

Asmodeous's tracking took him beyond the forest surrounding the castle and far to the southeast to a mountain range. *So, that was where they fled to.*

He recalled taking the path he now walked centuries prior, but as he crested a hill ahead, Asmodeous stopped in his tracks. Set into the side of the mountain ahead should have been a mighty fortress at the peak defensive design for its time. Its mighty walls should have overlooked a narrow passage through the mountains leading further south. However, the pass was completely buried under centuries of rock, and the keep was little more than a single ruined battlement.

He continued forward, still following Elias and Cecilia's trail. It would have made sense for them to flee to this fortress, but what happened to it?

Asmodeous's thoughts were interrupted when he spotted a van and several people milling about at the base of the ruined wall. There were numerous cameras set about, and the van had a large letter "H" painted on the side. *Perhaps they have some inkling as to what transpired here.*

Asmodeous began to approach, but a tall man in a thin jacket and a ball cap jogged over to meet him. He spoke in Romanian, "Uh, sir? I'm gonna have to ask you to leave. We're filming a historical documentary here."

A group of historians? Intriguing. "Might I speak with the historians on hand?" Asmodeous asked politely in Romanian, using Adam's voice.

"I'm afraid you can't, sir. Now be on your way," the man said dismissively.

"What happened here?" Asmodeous pressed, undeterred.

"Hey, can I get some help over here? This guy won't leave!" the man called over his shoulder in English.

He must think I do not understand. "I wish to know what occurred here, nothing more," Asmodeous insisted, also switching to English.

"Piss off, stranger!" another man spat, waving his hands as if to shoo Asmodeous away.

"If only you would let me speak with..."

"Are you deaf? He said piss off!"

How unfortunate. Asmodeous heaved a sigh. "So be it." He extended his will into the shadows throughout the area and called them to do his bidding. The crew screamed as the shadows gathered into waving tendrils around Asmodeous. He then proceeded to tear them all apart.

Once every human in the area was dispatched, Asmodeous sifted through the information they had gathered. Apparently, the documentary they were filming was concerning great historical mysteries, and they had chosen to film at the wall because no one knew anything about it.

Rythiel, you bastard. Asmodeous had no doubt who had erased Cecilia's family name from history. Worse still, the trail he had followed to reach here had vanished entirely. Whether its sources had perished here or had simply masked their escape, Asmodeous had no way of knowing.

For three days, he remained at the keep in an attempt to locate a trace of his followers, but all was in vain. Without a guide of some sort, he had no way of piecing together what had become of Elias or Cecilia.

However, there was more he could do in the meantime. Asmodeous closed his eyes, drifting through the screaming cold once again before he opened them to look upon his sarcophagus beneath Corbant Manor. He had not returned here since the night Cassandra had freed him. Her father's corpse, undiscovered by the authorities since the passage was re-sealed, lay as nothing but bones nearby. However, Asmodeous only had eyes for a little leather-bound journal lying next to his sarcophagus.

He recalled sending Cassandra's older sister, Allison, to retrieve it. She had done well before meeting her unfortunate demise. Still, her death had served him well in bringing Cassandra to him, and her spirit had served him even better by preventing Cassandra and Adam's escape. Though she was unwilling to participate, she was powerless to resist Asmodeous's compulsion, which had been all that prevented her from interfering in Kaleb's attempt at depravity.

Asmodeous picked up the journal before closing his eyes, reappearing on the mansion's front porch. In the light of early evening, he perused the journal. Most was commentary on the former owner's life as head doctor of an asylum. Eventually, Asmodeous came across a series of pages without any semblance of narrative or cohesion. The pages were strewn with distorted drawings of things both human and inhuman and everything in between. However, even Asmodeous's deadened heart leapt as he laid eyes upon a familiar symbol.

It was a simple eye with lashes drawn coming out of the top lid in the shape of fingers. *The Clawed Eye.* The symbol appeared repeatedly throughout that section of the journal, and Asmodeous almost laughed aloud with triumph. He closed his eyes once more, this time opening them to the looming shadow of Corbant Asylum.

The moment he crossed the threshold, Asmodeous felt a familiar cold. He followed the sensation to its source in a once-sealed chamber beyond a maze of lath and plaster. Asmodeous peered into the pit beyond the doorway, once covered by a rotted wooden floor, and saw the giant stone sarcophagus wrapped in chains and set into the wall at its bottom. The coldness emanated from it in waves, and in the deathly silence of the building around him, Asmodeous heard the familiar whispers issuing from it.

For the first time in five hundred years, Asmodeous laughed with delight. Somehow, miraculously, Madness had been entombed not even a day's walk away from where he himself had been imprisoned. Whatever his enemies' plans had been, they had made a fatal error.

Triumphant, he took his time returning to the front entrance of the asylum. As he walked through the building, his thoughts turned to what would happen next.

To overturn the natural order, unnatural power is necessary.

Madness was one source of that power. Now, Asmodeous needed to find the other four.

Despair, Anger, Madness, Doubt, and Fear.

As for where he would bring them together, all he needed was a location steeped in death...which he had in the form of Corbant Manor. After five and a half hundred years, he was now once again closing in on his endgame.

However, when Asmodeous passed through the doorway leading out of the asylum, he was surprised to find someone there waiting for him. It was a tall, darkly olive-skinned man in an elaborately embroidered black overcoat and a top hat.

"Elias?" Asmodeous asked, almost unable to believe his eyes. *He* had *survived.*

"Master? Is it really you?" Elias asked in reply, both his eyes and his accented voice unbelieving.

"It is I," Asmodeous confirmed. "What brought you to me?"

"I was looking for you, Master. Cassandra told me that you had been kept at Corbant Manor, but I didn't find you there, so I came here to see if I could pick up your trail. Truth be told, I hadn't expected to meet you here."

"Fate favors us this night, it seems. How did you come to meet Cassandra?"

"She had travelled to Chicago but had the unfortunate fate of being attacked on the streets. I saved her...in my fashion."

Perhaps she will remain useful for some time yet. "Where is she now?"

Elias smirked. "She had a personal matter to attend to."

Satisfied, Asmodeous asked, "What all has transpired in my absence?"

"Perhaps we should converse in the car?" Elias answered, gesturing toward an idling limousine beyond the front gate of the asylum.

Asmodeous shook his head with a subtle smile. "You seem to have done very well for yourself, Elias."

"I have had five hundred years to get my affairs in order, Master. I should hope so," Elias replied with a chuckle.

As they started toward the limousine, Asmodeous observed, "I trust then that we have a great deal to discuss."

Elias nodded with a satisfied smile. "That we do, and I trust you will be pleased, Master."